Penny-farthing Sally

Elizabeth O'Hara

POOLBEG

For Hannah

Published 1996
by Poolbeg Press Ltd
123 Baldoyle Industrial Estate
Dublin 13, Ireland

The Publishers gratefully acknowledge the support of The Arts Council.

A catalogue record for this book is available from the British Library.

ISBN 1 85371 686 3

Cover painting by Tom Roche
Cover design by Poolbeg Group Services Ltd
Set by Poolbeg Group Services Ltd in Garamond 10.5/13.5
Printed by The Guernsey Press Ltd,
Vale, Guernsey, Channel Islands.

ৼ

Praise for the Bisto Merit Award & RAI Award Winning
The Hiring Fair

"A lovely read . . . "
The Irish Times

"A moving story with a memorable heroine at its heart."
The Sunday Independent

ৼ

Praise for the Bisto Book of the Year
Blaeberry Sunday

"A bittersweet story of young love and its disappointments."
The Irish Times

" . . . A poignant, but unsentimental, portrayal of a
girl growing to understand the sacrifices involved in
asserting her independence."
The Irish times

About the Author

Elizabeth O'Hara is the pseudonym of Eilís Ní Dhuibhne, a well-known novelist and short story writer. Her books for children include *The Uncommon Cormorant, Hugo and the Sunshine Girl,* the best-selling Bisto Merit Award Winning *The Hiring Fair* and Bisto Book of the Year Award Winning *Blaeberry Sunday*.

Acknowledgements

Thanks to Bo, and to Nicole Jussek
and all at Poolbeg

Contents

Also by Elizabeth O'Hara

The Hiring Fair
Blaeberry Sunday

Published by Poolbeg

One

The Wardrobe

The cherry trees swayed, and showers of pink petals drifted silently to the ground. Under the sugary foam of blossom a gardener moved slowly back and forth. He was dressed all in black, and was carefully raking the gravel path. Even though it was raining, he had been raking for hours, as he always raked, clearing the petals, and etching long straight lines in the grey pebbles. Every day the wind and the children undid his work and every day he did it all over again.

Sally stood at the nursery window, watching. She liked to gaze at the figure of the gardener moving like a black beetle along the wide gravelled path. She liked the trees, ever changing – their bare black arms in winter, flung out against the sky, their spring veils of creamy buds, and now, in early May, their first blossoms and flowers, the pale green leaves which decked out the trees like new summer frocks. On fine days, she liked to see the women in their neat dark jackets and long slim skirts, their smart beribbonned hats – nurses or mothers – pushing perambulators along the winding path under the trees, while sailor suited boys and girls in blue pinafores wheeled hoops or threw spinning tops on the paths.

1

Most of all she liked to leave the nursery and go down to the park herself, to play with Snow, the oddly-named girl who was her pupil. But they would not be going today, unless the weather changed.

Snow was out somewhere with her mother – Sally's boss, Mrs Violet Erikson. Professor Erikson was at Trinity College, and Biddy, the cook and general maid, was at the grocer's shop in Rathmines.

Sally was alone in the big house. This seldom happened. She stretched, and breathed deeply. Her lungs filled with the nursery air – cool air, lightly flavoured with chalk and linseed oil and apples. Snow liked to munch apples as she worked, and a big bowl of them always stood on the table under the window.

Sally left the room and went out onto the landing.

Four closed doors faced her, like four wise old brown eyes.

She paused for a moment and listened. All was quiet. The afternoon had settled into the empty rooms of the house, filling every nook with its sleepy silence. "Shsh," the rooms seemed to whisper. "Shhsh! Shsh! We're resting. Do not disturb."

But Sally had wanted, for months, to see what Mrs Erikson's room looked like. Mrs Erikson was an unusual woman. She wore extraordinary, sometimes outrageous, clothes, and behaved like no other woman Sally had ever met. Was her own private room as exotic as she herself was?

Sally pushed open one of the solemn brown doors.

She stepped into Mrs Erikson's room.

At that very moment the sun, which had been hidden by rain all day, broke through a cloud. Suddenly the room was drenched with a flood of syrupy light. Sally rubbed her eyes, smiled, and gazed around.

A big square chamber, its long windows were draped in red velvet curtains, fringed with gold. In one window an

2

ornate brass pot held an enormous jungle-green aspidastra plant. A red Turkish carpet gleamed on the nutty wood of the floor and a big brass bedstead, its rails of black and gold looking like the bars of a fancy prison, stood somberly in the corner. There was a dressing table, cluttered with cut-glass jars and crystal bottles, with heavy brushes, their backs ornately twisted silver, their hairs bristling, thickly white. Two shining mahogany wardrobes stood at one end, like implacable sentries.

The most unusual feature, to Sally's eye, was the wallpaper. It was a dark midnight blue, and covered with a pattern of unicorns and ladies picked out in gold. Hanging on the wall just across from the bed were two tapestries, also depicting ladies, with thick manes of golden hair. They were dressed in flowing embroidered smocks and the tapestries were coloured with deep blues and crimsons, greens and golds. These lent the room an effect of ancientness and, yes, weirdness. Sally felt uneasy, amid all the pretty things, and not only because she knew she was taking a risk in being in this room at all. It was more than that: the mood of the room was from another world, stranger, older, odder, than even the eccentric world of the Erikson's household. She found herself breathing deeply, sucking the air of the real world into her lungs.

But she could not resist exploring further. She touched the thick, silk encrusted cloth of the tapestries and ran her hand over the embroidered unicorns. They felt as mysterious and lovely as they looked. She lifted up the cloth and looked at the underside of densely criss-crossed threads, knots and tangles. Here, you could see all the painstaking work that had gone into the creation of the rich, stylish picture that decorated the topside of the tapestry. Who had sat and sewed all this detail? How long had it taken them to do it?

3

Sally felt the rough texture of the behind the scenes stitching for a few minutes, imagining the women who had embroidered all the magical pictures. Then she moved on, and opened the doors of the first wardrobe.

The sharp, overpowering smell of mothballs almost knocked her down. A sea of grey and black serge met her gaze: Professor Erikson's suits.

She jumped back, partly in surprise and partly because of the strong smell. It was not what she had anticipated. She opened the second wardrobe.

Blue and gold and red and yellow. Silk and satin, spangle and glimmer.

A picture from a dream.

Fascinated, she reached for them.

Sally had been living with the Eriksons for many months. Some time ago her friend Geraldina Bannister had written to her in Donegal and told her that they were looking for a governess for their ten-year old daughter Snow – a governess who could speak Irish. Sally had eventually made up her mind to take the job. It had been a wrench, saying goodbye to her friends and family, and travelling as far away as Dublin. But she had been filled with curiosity, with a longing to move out into the big world. She had wanted to see new places and meet new people. And Geraldina had reassured her that the Eriksons would be good and kind employers.

"Could you believe anything that one would say?" Sally's mother had asked. "She's as mad as a hatter herself."

Sally agreed that Geraldina could be eccentric. But she trusted her judgement of character, and had decided to take the risk.

She had been away from home before anyway, when she worked as a hired girl on a farm in Tyrone. That had been an enormous adventure at the time. To her it had seemed that Tyrone was a foreign country, a million miles from home. And in many ways it had been like a foreign country: the language was different, the houses looked different, the people behaved in a different way from the people of Glenbra, her home.

But everything is relative. If Tyrone was a foreign country, Dublin was another planet.

She could still remember her wonder and amazement when she first arrived here, almost a year ago.

She had travelled alone on the train to Dublin. It had been the longest journey, by far, that she had ever made in her life, and it was a longer journey by train than most people in her family had ever made – when they travelled, it was by boat: to America, to Canada, or to Scotland. She had aunts and uncles in Philadelphia and Ontario, and her sister, Katie, was somewhere in Scotland – nobody knew quite where. But no member of the Gallagher family had ever gone to Dublin before, even for a visit.

All the way across Ireland she had kept her eyes glued to the window, anxious to see everything. Half of Ireland had swept past her gaze as the train chugged along. Pinch of pepper pinch of pepper went the wheels, pinch of pepper pinch of pepper. And Ireland flashed past.

What was it?

Fields. Fields, fields, fields. Slow meandering rivers, silver button lakes, little pudding hills, little drumlins. Small granite stations with men in black suits waving flags on the platform. Little towns, little houses. And fields, fields, fields.

Her first sight of Dublin had been Amiens Street Station. Iron everywhere. Clanking, noisy, grey iron. Steam billowing overhead. Churning wheels, thrashing pistons, coughing engines, piercing whistles. Everyone seemed to be shouting or even screaming. *Belfast train platform two! Tuppence a dozen the apples! Freeman's Journaaaal! Freeman's Journaaal!* That's what the voices were saying, among other things. But to Sally they all blended together in one overpowering, terrifying, roar. So this is Dublin, she thought, standing on the platform, letting her bag rest on the ground. Noisy and busy and full of hard hostile surfaces.

She felt lost and a bit frightened.

At the same time, a surge of happiness ran through her like an electric current. The station was full of energy. A human river flowed through it, a river of bustle and exuberance and work. It was exciting and thrilling, as well as daunting. She felt lost and alone, on the one hand. On the other she felt filled with power. Already after a few minutes she felt she liked this place. She felt she could rise to its challenge. She felt, in a way, at home.

In Amiens Street Station.

Biddy, the Erikson's servant, was there to meet her. Sally stood in the middle of the station, wondering where she was and how she would recognise her, when she caught sight of a woman with a cardboard placard saying "Erikson" standing at the gate for the train to Bray. It wasn't the most likely spot to pick if you were meeting someone getting off the northern train. But that, Sally soon learned, was not untypical of Biddy.

Sally walked up to her and extended her free hand. "Hello," she said. "I'm Sally."

"Glory be to God!" said Biddy. "I thought you'd never get here. I thought you were lost. I've been here this hour or more."

"The train just got in ten minutes ago," said Sally.

"Them old trains are always late, aren't they?"

"Well," said Sally, "yes."

The train had been on schedule.

Biddy was a plump lady with a round, apple face and

very blonde curls. Her curls were swept up on her head, under her little dark green hat, but a few of them had escaped and fluttered around her face, like Easter chicks. She was wearing a dark green jacket and matching skirt, and a white frilly blouse. Sally wondered what age she was: her face looked very fresh , but her hands were rough, with thick hard fingers. Probably she was about thirty, Sally thought.

"You're very welcome to the big city," Biddy said, when she had got over the shock of seeing Sally. "Did you have a nice journey?"

"Yes thank you," answered Sally.

She prepared to tell Biddy about it. But she didn't get a chance.

"I hate them old train journeys myself," said Biddy. "I get exhausted sitting for hours with nothing to do but stare out the window at old sheep and cows. I'm from the country myself more or less but even so I hate looking at all them fields for hours on end. Thanks be to God I got out of them is what I say."

"Where are you from?"

"I'm from Galway." Biddy replied. "They call it the city of the tribes but it isn't a real city at all after you've been to Dublin. I lived outside it anyway in a place called Roscahill, out in the country. Have you ever heard of Roscahill?"

Sally hadn't.

"It's a grand place but I don't mind telling you that I'm glad to be out of it. I've been in Dublin this fifteen year and more. And you're a real country lass, I can tell by the cut of you."

Sally put her hands to her face, embarrassed.

"Yes, you have that country look on you all right. Anyone can see that you're straight out of the bog. But never mind, that'll wear off after a few months in the bright lights and you won't know yourself. We'll soon smarten you up, never you fear. Now give me that little bag of yours and we'll go and catch a hackney and get home."

Sally handed over her small bag, which contained her books and clothes, without a word. Country girl? And she was wearing her very smartest outfit, the one which had been made specially for her mother's wedding only a few years ago. She'd even bought a new hat especially for Dublin – a flat navy boater, with a blue velvet ribbon round it. The lady in the shop had assured her it was the very latest thing.

Looking around the station, it was clear that it was not the latest thing in Dublin. Here, all the most visible ladies were dressed in a completely different style. Their skirts were straighter and slimmer than Sally's; their jackets were fitted tight to the skin. For hats they had tiny objects perched pertly on the crowns of their heads, sprouting the plumage of tropical birds. Not just the clothes and colours, but the shape of the women's very bodies seemed different from Sally's own shape, and, to her eyes, quite unnatural. They had tiny waists like wasps' and jutting pear-shaped bottoms, and their heads seemed to be out of kilter with their shoulders. Sally stared at them, in their flounces and feathers, their dipping, swooping laces and silks. What did they look like? Plump-breasted pigeons? The letter "S"?

"Or would you rather stop and have a cup of tea first?" Biddy interrupted Sally's musings, just as her eye caught a small fair-haired girl with bare feet, whose clothes were a collection of grey rags. The girl was singing in a lusty voice and a few people threw pennies at her. "Maybe you're thirsty after the journey? They do a nice scone and jam in the restaurant here and the Missus gave me a florin to spend on you if I needed it."

"Oh no, thank you," said Sally hurriedly. She had been travelling for ten hours and she really wanted to get to her new home.

"All right so," said Biddy.

She led the way out of the station and onto the street. A line of black carriages and jaunting cars stood at the edge of the pavement. There was a strong smell of horse dung. Clouds of flies hovered in the air, buzzing menacingly. Men wearing black hats and thick tweed suits leaned against the vehicles, or sat on their boxes. Some of them were chatting to one another and others stood in silence, brushing away the flies.

"Palmerston Park if you please," said Biddy to the man standing by the first car in the line. It was an enclosed cab.

"Right you are, madam," he said. He took the bags from Sally and Biddy. Then he opened the door of the cab and helped them sit inside.

Sally sat opposite Biddy in the dark enclosed space.

"Ah, this is the life!" said Biddy. "It's not often I travel by hackney cab, let me tell you, and you probably won't be using them much either."

"Oh? Why not?"

Sally felt a bit disappointed. She had not travelled in a vehicle like this before, ever, but she felt she would be happy to use one as often as possible. It felt very cosy.

"Not for the likes of us," said Biddy. "I've more to be doing with my hard earned money than splashing it out on cabs. These are for the gentry. I don't know what put it into the Missus's head to let us use one today."

"No," said Sally. "I don't know either."

Maybe she thinks I am a rather special person, is what she was thinking, though.

"How do you usually travel, then?" she asked.

"You're jokin' me?"

"No. I'd just like to know."

"Have you ever heard of shank's pony?"

"I can guess what that is."

"That's the main mode of transport for you and me, my dear. And there's the tram as well."

"Ah! Is that a tram?"

Sally pointed to a large vehicle, big enough to hold about twenty-five people. It moved in grooves and was linked by an antenna to an overhead cable. It had two decks, a closed one downstairs and an upper deck which was open to the air. At one end of the tram was a large staircase, leading from the platform where people got on and off to the upper deck. Although it was autumn at this time, and quite chilly, some people sat on top of the tram. By now they were on the quays, trotting along by the Liffey.

"That's an electric tram. I suppose you never saw the like of that before?"

"No."

The tram looked lovely. It was green and shining, and had huge advertisements on each side. Reckitt's Blue, said one, simply. The other was an advertisement for Epp's Cocoa.

"You're a real yokel aren't you? No mistake. That is a tram. The tram you'll be getting when you get one is the Number Twelve. That goes from Palmerston Park, just outside our hall door, as far as Nelson's Pillar, on Sackville Street. Thruppence is the fare. It's scandalous."

"Will we be passing Sackville Street today?"

"Well . . . we'll see it, when we turn up at Westmoreland Street. We'll see O'Connell Bridge and Nelson's Pillar and Dan O'Connell and all. Yes."

"Tell me the names of everywhere we pass, will you?" Sally implored her companion.

Biddy looked at her in amused consternation, as if she thought Sally were not all there. She screwed up her mouth to say something glib but then she looked out. They were passing the Four Courts. Two swans were swimming on the river.

10

"Of course I will, my dear," Biddy, who knew the name of the Four Courts, although not of much else, said.

Cabs, trams, horses, bicycles. Hats. Seas of hats, men's black bowlers, women's black and white, brown and straw. Flowers nodding and ribbons waving, feathers pluming. Horns honking, voices calling, hooves pounding, wheels cranking. Chimneys smoking. Beggars begging. Vendors vending. Children crying. Children laughing. Children playing. Children begging. Herds of cattle and sheep being driven down the streets, blocking the traffic and causing uproar. Flies everywhere and, in many places, a strong, putrid stench of sewage.

"The dung dodger!" Biddy cried, at one stage, pointing at a man pushing a handcart.

"What?"

"He goes around collecting the you know what from the back yards. Ugh, what a smell!"

That was on Harcourt Street. Sally pinched her nose and understood that life in a city posed problems that country people never dreamed of.

Palmerston Park was a sea of green, a quiet haven, after all the commotion of the city. The trees spread, their shadows making delicious pools of dark on the bright grass. Houses rose easily, gracefully, behind long gardens, full of roses and shrubs. Palmerston Park looked as if it had been there for a thousand years, as if it had all the space and time in the world. No bustle or hustle here.

That had been many months ago.

Now Sally had settled in. The house on Palmerston Park was home, more or less, to her. Its residents were known, at least in their outer habits. Mrs Erikson and the Professor, Snow and Sam, the son of the family who spent most of his time away at school, in England. Biddy in the kitchen. Jem and George and Mick, messenger boys who called with

11

groceries, or bread, or meat, nearly every day. The milkman with his cartful of silver churns.

Mrs Erikson dressed in lovely, exotic dresses. She loved the theatre and acted herself, sometimes. Sally knew many of her dresses quite well, by now, but she wanted to see them all.

She began to pull them out and lay them on the bed.

There was a gold kimono, with peacocks on it, and a silver dress made entirely of lace. There was a yellow crinoline with hundreds of tiers of frilly white ruffles sewn around the skirt, and an orange and black sari. Sally held the dresses up to the light. At first she held them to herself and looked at her reflection in the mirror. Then she started to put them on, one soft, caressing garment after the other.

She became a Japanese geisha girl, and a gentle Indian maiden going to her marriage ceremony. She was a flirt at the court of Louis the Fourteenth and a duchess in a feudal castle, waiting for her lord to return from the crusades. She was a princess, a queen, a dancer in the bazaar at Byzantium.

The pile of shimmering cloth grew, as Sally put on and then discarded one personality after the other.

Then she heard the iron gate creak. She was wearing a long robe of silver and white linen, with a blue cloak lined with ermine. She ran to the window. Mrs Erikson and Snow were walking up the path to the hall door.

Two

Rescued by a Poet

Sally ran back to the bed and looked in dismay at the huge heap of clothes that lay on it.

She pulled off the thing she was wearing and hung it hastily in the wardrobe. Then she grabbed a few other garments, pushed them onto the pink quilted hangers where they had been hanging until an hour ago – she had spent a whole hour in here, not noticing the time passing – and shoved them into the wardrobe. That took a few minutes. Only about fifty more dresses to go, she thought, pulling and shoving.

After one more dress she realised it would be quite impossible to get all the clothes back in the wardrobe in less than half an hour. And that's if she were lucky and efficient, which people rarely are when they are caught red-handed.

Sally felt like crying.

Mrs Erikson would be furious with her if she found her in here, going through the contents of her wardrobe. Even if she believed that Sally had not been stealing something – which was unlikely – she was going to take a very dim view of a girl who intruded in her bedroom, into her very wardrobe, as soon as her back was turned.

She had been so kind to Sally. Biddy had told her that she was a completely exceptional missus, making few demands on her employees and, in the case of Sally, going out of her way to make her feel happy in her surroundings.

Of course that was because she was half cracked, Biddy said, echoing Sally's mother's views of Geraldina Bannister. But you can't have everything.

In Sally's experience, some of the best people were those who were often described as "half cracked", so she was quite pleased to find herself employed by one.

But she did not think even Mrs Erikson was cracked enough to understand what she, Sally, was doing in her bedroom, going through the contents of her wardrobe.

Sally could hear Mrs Erikson and Snow in the hall. Mrs Erikson had excellent voice projection. Her voice was not always loud, but it could always be heard all over whatever place she happened to be in.

"Take off your coat dear and hang it on the hallstand!"

The words rang through the house.

"Where is Sally?" Snow asked, in her smaller, high pitched voice. At least that's what it sound liked from up here.

"You can go and find her in a minute, dear. I'm going to lie down . . . "

Sally picked up an armful of the clothes and shoved them in a bunch into the bottom of the wardrobe. She grabbed the rest of the clothes and stuffed them under the bed. Then she ran from the room, shutting the door behind her, and tiptoed across to the nursery.

When Snow came in two minutes later Sally was seated at the desk, writing a letter.

"Hello Sally, we had a great time in town," Snow said.

"Tell me all about it," said Sally.

"Can I tell you in English?"

14

Sally was employed to look after Snow in a general way, but also to teach her Irish.

It was easy to look after Snow in a general way, but it was not so easy to teach her Irish. Or anything. She was not a very studious girl.

"Well, you can tell me in English, just for once. And tomorrow you can tell me in Irish, when you are fresher."

If I am still in this house, thought Sally, which is not very likely, under the circumstances.

Snow started to tell Sally about her afternoon in town.

Sally listened with one ear. With her other she was attending to the movements of Mrs Erikson.

She heard a door banging downstairs, and waited for the footsteps on the stair.

"Then we went into Pim's and we looked at some new dolls they have just got in. Mamma will get me one for my birthday if I am good and study hard and learn Irish. So I don't suppose I'll get one really."

"Your birthday is a long way off," said Sally absently. There was no sound on the stairs. Could she have taken off her shoes and crept up so quietly that there was not a sound to be heard?

"The tenth of August. Not that far off, I'm afraid," said Snow, tossing one of her fair plaits off her shoulder. She was a demure, fair-haired girl, small for her ten years. Her complexion was snow white and she had large blue-grey eyes. She was wearing a simple white dress with a pale blue sash. Her mother liked her to wear white as much as possible. "That's the kind she is," Biddy had explained, in exasperation, to Sally. "She's the kind that gives her child a ridiculous handle of a name like Snow – I mean Snow, I ask you, did you ever in your life hear of man or beast with a name the like of that? – and then makes her wear dresses that match the name!"

15

"Didn't your mother go to lie down?" Sally could not stop herself asking this question.

"I don't know," said Snow, helpfully. "After we looked at the dolls we called on this friend of Mamma's who lives near Merrion Square and we had tea with him. He's doing some play that Mamma would like to be in but can't be because . . . I forget why. Because he doesn't want her to be in it or something . . . she was quite cross with him . . . "

Sally could hardly bear the tension. Mrs Erikson had still not come upstairs.

"Don't you want something to eat Snow? You must be starving."

"I just told you, we had tea with this man. Tea and madeira cake and bread and butter. Naturally I am not in the least bit hungry."

"I think I'll go down to the kitchen for something myself, then, if you can excuse me for a minute," said Sally. "I think I'd like a cup of tea."

She really needed one. Also, she thought she could ask Biddy to talk to Mrs Erikson and hold her up for as long as it would take her to put the clothes back properly.

On the way downstairs, she remembered that Biddy was out as well.

Maybe she had come back by now.

She decided to take a quick look in the kitchen anyway.

The kitchen was down in the basement of the house. To get there you had to go down the main staircase, then down the long hall to the back of the house, and then down another dark flight of stairs which led to the basements.

Sally sped along.

At the top of the cellar stairs she met Mrs Erikson.

"Ah, Sally, how are you?" the latter beamed. There were not very many women who would beam at their servants and ask them how they were. Mrs Erikson was one in a

16

million. Sally realised this very well now, when she was at risk of losing her, although she had just that morning been thinking that Mrs Erikson was a bit unreliable, nice one minute and nasty the next.

She was carrying a cup of tea in her hand.

"I'm fine thank you," said Sally. "Just popping down to Biddy for a minute."

"She's not there. She's still at the shops – you know Biddy, can't stop talking. I'm just going up to have a little rest before dinner. I've had such a stressful afternoon in town – I won't bore you with the details. Run along now my dear!"

Sally stepped heavily down to the kitchen as Mrs Erikson headed for the main staircase.

The doorbell rang.

"Oh dear, whoever can that be?" sighed Mrs Erikson. "Would you be a dear and answer the door for me, Sally? Thank you so much."

Sally raced back up the kitchen stairs and walked quickly to the hall door.

A very tall, dramatic-looking, man, with a shock of jet black hair and eyes like dark lakes, stood there. He was wearing a flowing cravat, in deep crimson silk, rather than the bow-tie most men wore, and he hummed to himself like a big bee as he stood on the doorstep.

"Hem, good afternoon," he said. "Is Mrs Erikson in?"

"Come in," said Sally, "I'll go and see."

Mrs Erikson had vanished into the library – the largest room in the house, and one of Sally's favourite places. It contained thousands of books, their rich dark red and green and blue spines covering all the walls like a tantalizing tapestry of stories.

"Who shall I say it is?" she remembered to ask.

"Oh, tell her it's Mr Yeats."

Mrs Erikson ran out into the hall.

"Willie!" she said. "Did you follow us home?"

"Yes, as a matter of fact I did," said the man called Willie, or Mr Yeats.

"So what is it?"

"Could I talk to you a little more please? Is that convenient at the moment?"

"It is *not* convenient," said Mrs Erikson, looking at him sternly. "I am completely exhausted and very, very unhappy. But I will make a special sacrifice and talk to you."

"Good," said Willie.

"This way," said Mrs Erikson, leading him into the library and pulling the door shut behind her.

Sally ran back upstairs and spent the next twenty minutes rearranging the dresses in Mrs Erikson's wardrobe. When she was finished it looked as if nobody had touched it. She went back to Snow.

"You were away for an awfully long time," said Snow.

"Yes," said Sally. "I'm sorry. I had to do something . . . Your mother has had a visitor."

"Oh, who?"

"His name is Willie."

"Oh yes. That's the man we called on in town. Willie Yeats. He writes poems and plays and things. He wouldn't let Mamma be in his play."

"I see. Well, perhaps he has changed his mind. Would you like to come over to the park?"

"Can we?"

"I think so. Just for a little while. Soon it'll be dark."

"Sam is coming home this evening, you know."

"He'll be here for dinner?"

"Yes. He's been struck ill, and he's coming home early for the long vacation."

"Isn't someone meeting him at the boat?"

18

"Yes. Pappa is."

"Oh?"

"If he can find the boat, that is."

Professor Erikson was the original absent minded professor. He could never find anything, not even his own shoes or socks, or his umbrella. He had not been born in Dublin or even Ireland, and, although he had lived here for fifteen years, did not yet know his way around any but a few streets. He knew the way from Palmerston Park to Trinity College, where he worked, and to the National Library, and to Kingsbridge Station, where he got the train to Kerry as often as he could. But he did not really know the way anywhere else.

"He'll get a hackney cab, I suppose," said Sally. "The driver will know the way."

"I hope so," said Snow. "Anyway, it will be nice to see Sam."

"Yes, it will," said Sally. "Let's have a quick walk, then, before the sun goes down."

They put on their jackets and hats and gloves, and crossed the road to the park.

Three

Sam and the Boers

The Eriksons were gathered around the dining-room table, drinking coffee.

Sally, who had eaten her dinner in the kitchen with Biddy, had been invited in to join them, in order to meet Sam on his first evening at home.

Professor Erikson was at one end of the table. Although he behaved like a professor and was one of the most learned people in Ireland he did not look like one. Indeed his appearance was that of a prize fighter, or an all-in wrestler: he was a huge, burly man, with thick grizzled curly hair and hands that looked more like the paws of some enormous animal, a bear or a panda, than of a man who spent all his time reading and writing books. The only thing that gave him away were his spectacles, perched half way down his large pug nose. These did not lend his face an air of learned dignity. But they did suggest that he belonged to a profession which attracts short sighted people. And as everyone knows, the profession of teaching, and especially of professing, is one of those.

Professor Erikson was, Sally knew by now, one of the gentlest and kindest men in the world. Although he was, as Mrs Erikson and Biddy had told her several hundred times, a very important and learned man, he was a country farmer at heart. He came from Norway. The stories he sometimes told about his childhood there reminded Sally of life in Glenbra.

"Hello Sally, how are you?" said Sam.

"How do you do, Sam?" asked Sally politely. She had only met Sam once before, when he had been home for Christmas, and had not got to know him. He was a quiet boy, and had spent most of his time alone in his room.

Sam looked younger than his seventeen years. He was tall but painfully thin, with fine fair hair falling in a fringe over his forehead. His face was bony and his skin pale, almost transparent. He always looked washed out, but tonight his complexion had a greenish pallor. You could tell that he had been sick. Against this skin, his mouth was luridly red. Mrs Erikson had just the same kind of mouth.

"Have some coffee, Sally?" Mrs Erikson motioned her to sit down at the table. There were two spare chairs and Sally sat self-consciously on one of them. Biddy, who was standing somewhere in the shadows, came forward and poured her a cup of coffee from a heavy silver pot. She made a small mock bow and raised her eyebrows at Sally as she did this.

"We have been talking about South Africa," said Mrs Erikson. "Sam is very interested in what is going on there."

"Oh yes?" said Sally. "What is that?"

"There is a conflict of interest between the English and the Boers."

"Oh?" Sally had not been reading the newspapers and did not know anything about this. "Who are the Boers?"

"The Boers are Dutchmen, who have lived in South Africa for more than three hundred years. They naturally don't like the idea of the English trying to move in and tell them what to do."

"The Boers won't give basic civil rights to any foreigners

in their republic," said Sam angrily. "You can't even vote in the Boer Republic if you are not forty years of age."

"Forty, and white, and a man," added Mrs Erikson, one of whose many interests was the "Votes for Women" question. She belonged to an organisation called The Irish Women's Suffrage and Local Government Association, which aimed to obtain for women the same voting rights as men. So far the efforts of the organisation had been unsuccessful, although they had made some small progress.

"And the English want everyone to be able to vote?" asked Sally innocently, "Even women?"

"You must be joking," said Mrs Erikson. "The English want to get their hands on the gold and diamonds that are in these places. The biggest gold and diamond mines in the world are there."

"That's not really true, Mamma," Sam's face was taut. He was trying hard to be patient. "The English in South Africa have always tried to make conditions better for everyone. Even for the blacks. And the Boers have always opposed them. They are terrible people."

"So are the English," said Mrs Erikson, who considered herself to be an Irish patriot as well as an ardent Suffragette.

"They are not!" exploded Sam. "They are the most civilized nation on earth. They are always trying to improve conditions everywhere for poor deprived people."

"First they make them poor and deprived and then they try to help them. And they never succeed."

"They are better than the Boers, anyway. The Boers in South Africa have written in their laws that the native Africans, any coloured people, are unequal to whites, and that they will never be equal."

"But can they be, really?" asked Mrs Erikson, in the penetrating tones that discouraged contradiction. "I mean really? Isn't their culture at such a low level?"

"The Bantu-speaking tribes are extremely civilised," said Professor Erikson, who had paid little attention to this conversation so far. He was not interested in politics, but he was interested in native Africans. "The Sotho and the Nguni have been making tools and weapons from iron for centuries. They are among the most interesting peoples of the world."

"It's not the same," said Mrs Erikson. "Is it? Tools and weapons made from iron? They are illiterate. They don't have trains or electricity or telephones."

"Do you think such things are the hallmarks of civilisation?" asked her husband.

"Well . . . I'm playing devil's advocate."

"I'd love to go to South Africa," said Sam, eyeing his mother warily. He did not want to witness one of her full-scale arguments with his father on his first night home.

They all laughed. He looked so eager.

"Don't be absurd, dear," said Mrs Erikson, patting him on his head and dismissing thoughts of civilisation from her own. "You are much too young to go anywhere – anywhere like that."

"I'm seventeen," said Sam, firmly.

"Are you really?" Mrs Erikson stared at him. "It seems only yesterday that you had long ringlets and a little dress."

"Ha ha, a little dress!" mocked Snow. "Little ringlets! Little sissy!"

"Anyway," pronounced Mrs Erikson, ignoring Snow's contribution to the conversation. "There may be trouble down there soon. So I read in the paper."

"That's why I would like to go," said Sam.

"My brave little soldier! That school in England is giving you strange ideas, I'm afraid. I think perhaps we should have kept you here."

"I'm glad you didn't," said Sam. "I am proud to be English."

There was a silence around the table, while everyone gazed at him.

"Don't be ridiculous, Sam. You are Irish, not English."

"Being born in a stable doesn't mean you're a horse," said Sam, smugly.

"This isn't a stable," said Mrs Erikson. "This is Ireland. Your father is Norwegian, your mother is Irish, you were born in Dublin. How can you imagine you are English?"

"I don't. But my loyalty is to the crown."

"It is not how many of the Irish feel," said Professor Erikson. "Most people in this country support the Boers, and I can understand why."

"Well, I can't," said Sam, hotly.

"This English school has gone to your head completely," Mrs Erikson sighed.

"He's just a little boy, who used to have ringlets and a dress," said Snow, giving Sam a shove in the ribs. "He doesn't know what he thinks."

"Exactly," said Mrs Erikson. "And next year you will be living here again, safely at home."

"I don't want to go to Trinity," said Sam. "I want to go to Oxford. I think it's better."

"Why?" asked Professor Erikson, who worked in Trinity.

"It's older," said Sam.

"Not much," said Professor Erikson.

"It is," said Sam, who was not quite sure how old either university was.

"A minute ago you wanted to go to South Africa," said Snow.

"Do shut up, Snowman," Sam turned away from his little sister.

Sally drank her coffee, mildly embarrassed by this family dispute.

"Well, Sally," said Mrs Erikson. "Now you have met Sam. Perhaps you have something to do upstairs?"

Sally took the hint and left.

She went down to the kitchen, where Biddy was engaged in washing up.

"I'll help you with that if you like," said Sally.

"All right. If you're not afraid to roughen your lily white hands."

"Why should I be?" Sally glanced at Biddy. She was red in the face from the steam, and tired.

"Oh, you're one of the toffs now!"

"I've worked on a farm and I've worked as a hired girl," said Sally.

"But now you're drinking coffee with the gentry, if you don't mind. I was always told by my mother, God be good to the poor woman, never to rise above my station."

"It was just once, Biddy. Usually I don't drink coffee at all, do I?"

"Still, you're doing rightly. Teaching that Snow one for a few hours a day, doing whatever you like the rest of the time. Lady Muck! Sure it's well for you, so it is. You've got it all sewn up. And you're well paid for it into the bargain, I'm thinking."

"Ten pounds a year, if you must know."

"There ye are! I get eight pounds and for that I'm slaving from dawn to dusk. Up at six in the morning and here breaking me back till nine or ten most nights."

"It's hard. I know what it's like, Biddy. I've done it myself."

"And what happens at the end of it all?" Biddy warmed to her theme. Her curls stuck to her forehead and her face grew redder than ever. "I'll be working until I can't work anymore, and then they'll dump me into the poorhouse like a worn-out nag."

"I'm sure that won't happen to you, Biddy."

"It happens to a lot like me. There's poor Miss Byrne across the road, she was with the Brownes for forty years. And then last year when she got so bad with rheumatism that she couldn't scrub any more the boot is what she got. Thirty pounds and the outside of the door. And do you know where that poor woman is now?"

"No." Sally felt her heart sink. Stories like this drained all the optimism out of her, and the world seemed to be full of such tales of woe.

"The South Dublin Union. Poor Miss Byrne that wore a fresh white blouse every day of her life stuck in that kip of a place. You wouldn't put a dog in it."

Biddy paused. Sally closed her eyes, trying to overcome the mixture of sadness and anger that was overwhelming her.

Biddy spoke in a calmer voice.

"I went in to visit her my last half day."

"And?"

"She was crying. She was sitting in this big ward full of all kinds of creatures, I wouldn't start to tell you what they're like. Tears rolling down her cheeks. She won't last the winter."

"It's very sad."

"It is. And that's what happens to most of us."

"It won't happen to you, Biddy. The Eriksons would never do anything like that to you. They like you too much."

"Sure there's no guarantee that I'll be with them forever, is there? I'm a good fifteen years younger than herself, not to speak of him. Methusaleh up the stairs."

"Someone will marry you soon."

"There's little likelihood of that, alanna. Sure I seldom meet a sinner in a pair of breeches, let alone marry one of them."

26

"Oh dear," said Sally. "Maybe I'm in the same boat myself."

"I doubt it," said Biddy, sceptically. "Here's a towel for you. Start drying."

Sally helped Biddy for an hour or so and then went upstairs.

She wrote two letters, one to her mother and one to her sister Katie in Scotland. She sent the letter to the farm in Ayrshire where Katie had been working a year and a half ago. It was the only address for her that she possessed.

Her correspondence with Katie had been erratic. Katie was not much of a letter writer and, when Sally sat down and thought about it, she realised that she hadn't heard from her in over a year. Her mother hadn't either.

The last time she had seen her, Katie had been home for a week. She had spent a summer picking potatoes in Scotland, and then had got a job there, as a servant at a farmhouse in Ayrshire. Sally had written to the address and Katie had written a few brief letters during her first few months there, telling Sally that she was well and that the family she worked for were kind. But she had stopped answering Sally's letters.

Talking to Biddy about the unhappy lot of servant girls reminded Sally that Katie was in the same position as Biddy. Or in an even worse position, since she was far away, in another country.

She wrote to her, telling her about Dublin and her new job, and urging her to write back soon.

She had not thought about her sister in half a year. But suddenly she missed her very much.

Four

The Countess Kathleen

A few days after Sam's homecoming Sally was in the nursery with Snow.

"I really hate this," Snow was saying. "Can't we go to the park?"

"No," said Sally. "But if you read these two pages you can have your tea and biscuits as soon as you've finished. And then we can do some painting for the rest of the morning."

Snow groaned. She turned back to the pages of the book and began to read in her appalling accent.

Sally looked at her with a mixture of amusement and despair. She was beginning to feel that teaching Snow was an impossible task. Snow had told her that she had had ten governesses already, and Sally wondered what had happened to the others.

Snow had read one sentence, very painfully, when Mrs Erikson burst into the nursery.

"Good morning, dears," she said. She was wearing a yellow dress, with bright brass buttons, and looked like a ray of middle aged sunshine.

"Good morning Mamma," said Snow, with a huge smile. Any interruption to work was always welcome as far as she was concerned.

"I just wanted to let both of you know, we are going to the theatre tonight," she said, breathlessly.

"That's good," said Snow, not very enthusiastically.

"You're coming too, Sally," said Mrs Erikson.

"Thank you very much, ma'm," said Sally. "That's very kind of you."

"What's the play?" asked Snow, suspiciously.

"It's Willie Yeats's new play," said Mrs Erikson. "It's called *The Countess Kathleen*. I thought I should play the leading role, and was disappointed when he told me that other day that it was already rehearsed and that his friend Maud Gonne was in it. It's ridiculous. The woman has a pretty face but she can't act to save her life. However, ours is not to reason why . . . I must say I think the man could have told me earlier . . . "

"People never tell you in time, Mamma, do they?"

"No. Anyway, let bygones be bygones. He has sent around four tickets for tonight's performance."

"Four?"

"Yes. You, me, Sam and Sally. Of course Pappa won't come. You know what he thinks of Willie."

"'That man is a pretentious bore'," quoted Snow. "That's what I think too. I bet it's a very boring play."

"I think it will be quite, quite wonderful," said Mrs Erikson. "Anyway, you are coming whether you like it or not. We'll leave the house at a quarter past seven, Sally. Please make sure than Snow is dressed and ready."

"Yes, ma'm," said Sally.

The play was in the Antient Concert Rooms in Brunswick Street.

Sally and the Eriksons went there on a sidecar.

It was still bright. The suburban roads were lined with cherry and almond blossom trees. The chestnuts were covered with tiny bunches of bright green leaves. All along

29

Rathmines Road young people – soldiers from Portobello barracks and young women – walked up and down. The soldiers walked on one side of the street and the girls on the other, mostly. From time to time a soldier crossed and joined one of the small groups of girls.

People were still strolling on the city streets as well. Although it was early May the weather was very dry and warm, and many people had changed into their summer clothes. The pavements were colourful with light dresses and hats, and the striped blazers of the more daring young men.

The foyer of the Antient Concert Rooms presented an equally colourful spectacle.

A huge crowd of people had assembled to see the first night of the new play, *The Countess Kathleen*, which was WB Yeats's first play.

The people thronged the foyer, greeting each other and talking. Some were dressed very grandly, in silk and satin evening gowns, while others had come in any old thing, it seemed to Sally.

Mrs Erikson spotted her friend Willie almost as soon as they stepped into the theatre.

"Look, there he is! That's Lady Gregory with him. I must go over and have a chat!"

It was obvious that Willie and Lady Gregory were being accosted by about half the people in the crowd, and there seemed to be very little chance of having a word with him. But Mrs Erikson battled her way through the mob.

It took about ten minutes to get to Willie.

"Hello," she said. "We managed to get here after all! The best of . . . "

But before he could hear what she was saying, a porter started to ring a bell, and the crowd surged to the door of the concert room.

Sally and the Eriksons took their places in the theatre. It

surprised Sally to see a lot of policemen coming in as soon as the audience sat down, and taking up positions all around the concert room.

"Do policemen always come to plays?" she asked Snow.

"Oh yes, always," declared Snow. "They are very interested in drama."

Snow often said the first thing that popped into her head. Facts did not concern her one way or the other.

The play was a little late in starting, but at last it did.

The lamps were turned down in the concert room. The curtain on the stage began to rise.

As soon as this happened all the noise in the auditorium came to a stop, as if a giant hand had been clapped over all the mouths that had been chattering madly until a second previously.

The curtain slowly rose.

The stage was revealed.

Sally gasped.

It was a country kitchen. An old man and woman and a young man sat by the fire, talking or about to talk.

It looked exactly like her kitchen at home, except that you could see that it was made of wood and cardboard.

The play was about the young man, whose name was Michael. He was planning to marry a girl called Delia, who was considered a good match by his parents, mainly because her uncle was a priest.

"I do be thinking sometimes, and Delia's uncle a priest, that we might be put in the way of making Patrick a priest some day, and he so good at his books," the mother, Bridget, said.

Patrick was not in the play but he was obviously their other son. Where was he? In some other room, reading maybe, Sally thought.

The old couple and Michael discussed the wedding, and how it was going to make them richer and better off. They

31

believed that marriage was about money, not about love or happiness.

Everything they said reminded Sally of things she had heard at home. Some of the things they said reminded her of what Biddy had been telling her the night before. The mother in the play was even called Bridget, and Sally felt guilty, for a minute, remembering that Biddy wasn't here and she was. Biddy was at home cleaning, or washing up, probably, while she was sitting at the play in the Antient Concert Rooms.

"If I brought no fortune I worked it out in my bones," Bridget in the play said, "laying down the baby Michael that is standing there now on a stook of straw, while I never dug the potatoes and never asked big dresses or anything but to be working."

When she said these lines something strange happened.

The audience had been quiet as mice. But suddenly a group of people began to hiss.

"Boo!" they called. "Boo! Shame! Shame!"

A few of the policemen moved over to the seats where the noise came from. And all was quiet for a while.

The play, which was quite short, progressed.

A strange old woman came to the house.

She was very tall, and wrapped from head to toe in a black shawl. You couldn't see her face.

"That's her," hissed Mrs Erikson to Sam, in a whisper which the whole theatre could hear. "Maud Gonne."

The woman in the black shawl told the family that she had lost all her friends and that she needed people to support her.

"Stiff, isn't she?" whispered Mrs Erikson.

"Shh!" said about fifty people, including Snow, Sam, and Sally. It was unbearably embarrasing.

Maud Gonne did not hear. She continued to talk about

32

the terrible things that had happened to her. She talked so persuasively that before the play ended, Michael changed his mind about marrying Delia and decided to follow her, the old woman in the black shawl.

He followed her out the door.

His parents were very upset (not half as upset as Delia would be when she found out, Sally thought). But when they asked the neighbours if anyone had seen an old woman they were told that she had not been seen. But a young beautiful woman had walked out of the cottage, looking like a queen.

When the play was over and the actors came to take their bow, the old woman pulled off her shawl. And underneath was a very tall, beautiful, young woman, with enormous blue eyes and golden red hair. She looked like a goddess. Everyone cheered very loudly when she revealed herself. It was uplifting to see someone who looked so perfect.

"Can't act," said Mrs Erikson, frowning. "A mistake."

When the actors were bowing, the people who had booed during the performance started to boo again.

They stood up and stamped their feet on the floor.

"Thomas Davis!" they chanted. "Remember Thomas Davis. Thomas Davis! Thomas Davis!"

A troop of policemen moved in on them and pulled them out of the theatre.

"Who are they?" asked Sally, as they walked out.

"Gaelic Leaguers," said Mrs Erikson. "Stupid young men."

"Why are they doing that?"

"I really do not know," said Mrs Erikson. "They don't like the play, or they don't like Yeats, I suppose. We'll find out soon enough."

They went out to the foyer during the intermission: a second play was to be performed afterwards. Everyone was gathered there again. They were saying how wonderful the play was, what fine performances the actors had given. But mainly they were talking about the disruptions.

"Beardless wonders from Trinity," said one fat man. "It's a slur on Irish women, they say. The Irish peasants never think about filthy lucre or such ignoble matters."

"And they never give birth to babies in stooks of straw!" said the woman who was standing next to him.

"My dear, you shock even me!" said her husband.

"Well, it will draw plenty of attention to the play anyway," said Mrs Erikson.

"Yes indeed. Some say that Yeats planned the whole thing. That he asked the students to come and protest and then asked the RIC along to throw them out. He remembers the riots that took place during Synge's Playboy a few years ago, and wants some of the same kind of notice for himself."

"He could hardly be that devious, could he?"

"Could he not? Our darling Willie!"

"You mustn't pay any attention to what people say," said Mrs Erikson to Sally, Sam and Snow, as they drove home in the dark streets after the second play, *The Heather Field*. "It is the duty of a first night audience to slander everyone involved. They all love Willie really. Did you like the play?"

She hadn't addressed Sally in particular but Sally, lost in memories of the night, answered.

"I thought *The Countess Kathleen* was wonderful," she said. "It was the best thing I have ever seen."

"I knew you'd like it," said Mrs Erikson.

"I thought it was boring," said Snow, yawning. "I knew it would be and it was. I'm so tired."

"It was all right," said Sam. "The fellow who played Peter was really funny, I thought. I liked him. But I liked *The Heather Field* more. I thought that was by far the better of the two plays."

Five

Sally joins the Gaelic League

Soon after her visit to the theatre, Sally was contacted by her old friend Geraldina Bannister, who had spent a summer learning Irish in Glenbra a few years earlier, and who had recommended Sally to the Eriksons.

Sally had had some contact with her since coming to Dublin, but not all that much. Geraldina, however, had promised, or threatened, to take her along to the branch of the Gaelic League to which she belonged several months earlier. Now she called around to fulfil her promise.

"I've been so terribly ill all winter," she said. "I got the flu and then several relapses. I haven't been myself for months."

Geraldina was looking thin and drawn, but otherwise she seemed in her usual high spirits.

Sally met her at the town hall in Rathmines just as the big clock struck eight, and they walked along the street.

It was still quite busy. Bicycles and a few cabs sped along, and the tram screeched and shuttled towards Rathgar. People dressed up for the evening strolled along the footpath; girls in white dresses linked arms with men in straw hats. People walked slowly, stopping to examine the shop windows: MacDonnell's and Byrne's, where many kinds of tea were displayed in copper urns; O'Reilly's the haberdasher, with its display of ribbons, elastics, spools of thread, and Browne the draper, where the latest fashions were displayed on plaster models.

Sally would have liked to linger and examine the summer frocks and hats, but Geraldina hurried her along.

The meeting was held in a shabby house up a lane off the main street. They knocked on the flaking door. Nobody answered and so Geraldina pushed. The door was open and in the dim light they climbed a bare wooden stairway. In a gloomy room lit by a very smelly gas lamp about twenty people were assembled.

They sat around on stacking chairs. Some of them were wearing their coats. Although it was quite warm outside, the atmosphere in the dingy room was damp and chilly.

The walls were covered in a grimy brown paper, which was peeling off in several places. Large damp spots like maps of the world covered the ceiling. The floor was bare and a bit dirty.

Sally didn't like it at all. She was used to much more attractive surroundings than this.

The people themselves, however, were much more appealing than the room. Many of them were young and enthusiastic, and they were all very friendly towards her.

They sat and chatted amongst themselves, some of them smoking cigars. Geraldina introduced Sally to a girl of about her own age called Ethel.

"I'm from Rathgar," Ethel said. "I've been a member for two months and I know heaps of Irish already. But I really joined for the fun."

Ethel was a small girl with brown hair, cut in a fringe. She had freckles on the bridge of her nose and was wearing a lovely dress: a white flowered muslin pelisse, or oversmock, over a pale blue skirt. She looked about twelve but was much older.

"What sort of fun do you have?"

"All kinds. We have ceilis and we have a cycling club and a walking club. And we're going to do a play. It's all great fun. This is my friend Thomas."

Sally said hello to Thomas, who struck her, at this first encounter, as being so completely average that there was nothing to say about him. Brown hair, ordinary face, average build.

"Where are you from? Have you been here before?"

"No," said Sally. "This is my first time."

At that moment the meeting was called to order by a man with black curly hair and small gold glasses.

He spoke only Irish. He welcomed everyone and told them they were going to have a special honoured guest later that night.

The meeting progressed – an agenda was read, and then letters were read aloud, and minutes read and passed. Sally had not been to a committee meeting before, so it was all new and interesting to her. They talked about what they had done since the last meeting and what they would do before the next one. Mainly they seemed to talk about raising money to keep the whole thing going. A second major problem was recruiting new members.

"We have already got a very large membership," the man in the glasses said. "But we must not be complacent. We must get more. Has anyone any ideas?"

People had. They had a lot of ideas, which another man, who was the secretary, wrote down in his notebook.

And so it went on, until the meeting was over and everyone got tea.

At that point the honoured guest was introduced.

His name was Douglas Hyde.

He was a small man with black hair and a huge walrus moustache. Sally did not think he looked very important, but he was. Everyone shushed and gasped and seemed delighted to see him.

He spoke to the group for about ten minutes, telling them that they were doing very good work and that he hoped they would continue. He said that what they were doing was the most revolutionary thing that had ever happened in the history of Ireland, and that the people of the future would recognise that and be grateful to them. He said they were saving the ancient culture of Ireland for the generations of the future and that nothing was more important.

He spoke with a lisp, but with such enthusiasm and conviction that everyone hung on every word, and clapped violently when he had finished.

Then they all got a cup of tea and two biscuits.

"He was marvellous, wasn't he?" said Ethel.

"Yes," said Sally.

"It's wonderful to see him in the flesh. I've heard so much about him," she went on. "Our founder." She closed her eyes. Then, changing the subject abruptly, she said "will you come cycling with us on Sunday?"

"Oh," said Sally. "I . . . "

Sally hardly knew what to say. The invitation was very sudden.

"Thank you," she said. "But I haven't got a bicycle."

"You haven't got a bicycle? That's terrible. Cycling is the best thing in the world, isn't it Thomas?"

"Well, it is quite amusing," said Thomas, smiling.

"I don't know how to cycle," said Sally, backing up her excuse. She did not really think she would have time to go cycling anyway.

"Oh dear, oh dear," said Ethel. "How dreadful for you. Don't they cycle much, where you come from?"

"Not much," said Sally. "Not at all, really."

"Where *do* you come from?" Ethel asked. She was a direct and forthright girl, who always asked what she wanted to know.

Sally was beginning to feel a bit out of her depth. Ethel obviously did not quite understand that Sally was not a young lady like her, with a lot of free time and probably a lot of money. But she did not know how to explain it.

"I come from Donegal," she said. "Some people there . . . that is, I have seen one or two bicycles there . . . but I have never had one myself."

Ethel and Thomas exchanged a look.

"I see," said Ethel. "Well, that's unfortunate. We have such fun, on our cycles."

"Where do you go?"

"Where *don't* we go is a better question!" Ethel laughed. "Everywhere. Last week we went to Blessington, and next week we will go out to Loughlinstown, and we've been to Howth and to Swords and all kinds of interesting places."

"Is it easy, cycling?"

"Very easy, when you know how," said Thomas. "Can I get you another cup of tea?"

"Oh yes, please," said Sally.

He went off to the table where the teapot stood.

"Maybe we could lend you a bicycle," said Ethel. "My mother has one that she hardly ever uses. It's a little old fashioned . . . "

"I couldn't dream of it," said Sally.

"No, really, I think you should try."

"But I've just met you!" Sally protested.

"That's true . . . but does it matter?" said Ethel.

Geraldina bounced up.

"I've put your name down for an audition for the play," she said to Sally.

"You've what?"

"They're going to do a play. It's one that Douglas Hyde, the man you heard speaking there, wrote. I forget what it's called now. I thought you'd be ideal for a part in it."

"But . . ."

Sally knew that Geraldina did not consult people before making decisions for them. Nevertheless she felt taken aback at the abruptness of this.

"No buts. You'd like to be in a play, wouldn't you?"

"I don't know. I've never thought of it . . ."

"You look so perfect for the sort of plays they are putting on now. That sort of Irish peasant look. Doesn't she look like the typical Irish peasant?" Geraldina addressed herself to Ethel.

"I'm not sure. What does a typical Irish peasant look like?"

"Like Sally. Black hair, blue eyes. That sort of mysteriously sorrowful look. She would have been a great Countess Kathleen."

"Half the women in Dublin think they would be a great Countess Kathleen."

"Most of them would be better than Maud Gonne."

"I think she is the most beautiful woman in Dublin."

"She can't act, though."

"Does that matter? In that sort of play?"

"Yes. It always matters. So, Sally, you should come here on Thursday night at eight o'clock for the audition."

"I'm not sure if I can . . ."

"Of course you can. I'll talk to Violet and fix it all up for you. Shall we go home now?"

"All right. Goodbye, Ethel."

Thomas came back with the tea.

"Oh dear, I'm sorry, I have to leave now. I'd forgotten all about the tea."

"Not to worry. I'll drink two cups," said Thomas. Sally smiled gratefully at him.

"Shall we see you on Sunday morning then?" Ethel asked.

"Oh, I don't know . . . " said Sally.

"Do come!" said Thomas. "You will enjoy it tremendously."

"What time?"

"We meet at ten o'clock, at the Town Hall."

"If I can, I will," said Sally, "goodbye now!"

Sally was relieved to be escaping from this situation.

"Where do you live?" called Ethel, as Sally moved towards the door.

"Oh, 89 Elmtree Park!" Sally said quickly, knowing, as she said it, that it would give rise to further misunderstandings.

Geraldina and Sally walked back to Palmerston Road together.

It was ten o'clock but just starting to get dark.

"I'm sorry not to have seen more of you" said Geraldina. "I feel quite guilty about it, since I am responsible for bringing you to Dublin."

"I've been very well," said Sally. "I am glad I took your advice and came here."

"Good. Nevertheless, I should have been more careful about maintaining contact."

"You've been ill . . . " Sally's voice trailed off. She was feeling tired, and could not think of anything more comforting to say.

"True, true. I've been ill. And I've had my cousin to stay, my cousin who has been in the Congo."

"The Congo?"

"In Africa, yes."

"I hear so much about Africa these days."

"It is harrowing to listen to what he has to report. The way the Congo natives are treated is shocking."

41

"Oh?"

"By the rubber planters. They use natives to collect rubber, rubber for all the bicycle and automobile tyres and so on that we use in this part of the world. They pay them very little and if they don't collect enough they chop off their hands."

"Oh Good Lord," gasped Sally. "It can't be true."

"It is. My cousin has seen it with his own eyes."

Sally sighed deeply. The trees rustled in the dark, and she felt cold.

"But I am sorry, my dear, to trouble you with these gloomy stories."

"It is interesting," protested Sally, weakly.

"I must tell you all about my cousin on some future occasion. I promise to be more faithful about visiting you from now on."

"That would be lovely," said Sally. "Anyway, I'll see you at meetings of the Gaelic League."

"Yes, of course you will, my dear. And look, you are home! How charming the house is!"

The curtains had not been drawn and lamps glowed in several windows of the Eriksons' house, casting a mild yellow light on the lawn. The whole place looked homely, warm and welcoming.

"Yes, it is, isn't it?" agreed Sally. Suddenly she could hardly wait to get inside.

Six

Letters

Sally had a nightmare.

She was in a jungle. High spikey dark green leaves hemmed her in, but she battled her way through them. She was looking for someone: Manus. She knew he was somewhere in the jungle and if she kept looking she would find him. In the dream she was convinced of this, but also frustrated because she knew she had just missed him. One minute earlier he had been here. And she had missed him, somehow, by coming too late. By falling asleep too late, perhaps, or entering this dream too late.

She hacked through the thick foliage. Birds, coloured blue and green and yellow, flew away from her, screaming loudly and flapping their wings ferociously.

She came to a clearing.

There were three grass huts in the clearing, with small fires in front of each one. There were objects – stone querns, axes, vessels made of pottery – lying around. The doors of the huts were open – there were no doors, just holes, as entry ways. Lying outside one of the huts was a heap of material, silk and satin, blue and yellow and green, like the feathers of the birds. Sally walked over and picked up a length of blue cloth and draped it over her body. She knew Manus was in the hut.

When she walked to the door, she saw a string of cut off hands draped around the straw roof, like the stone-weighted ropes they used to tie down thatch at home.

She woke up.

Her room was full of morning light.

Manus was a boy – a young man now – in Donegal. She had not thought of him for a long time, for more than a year, although once she had been deeply in love with him.

For all she knew, he was married to some other girl by now. What was the name of that girl he used to walk out with, after her? She couldn't even remember.

The dream filled Sally with strange anxieties, but she laughed to herself when she considered how much she had cared about Manus, how she had thought of him every minute of the day, and how now she could hardly remember anything about him. He hadn't been on her mind even once in ages.

Did the dream mean anything?

Probably not. Sally did not really believe in dreams. The hands had come straight out of her conversation with Geraldina the night before. Manus had come from something that happened recently too. She just couldn't remember what.

"Do you dream, Snow?" she asked Snow that morning, when they were ensconced in the nursery.

"Yes," said Snow. "I dream the most vivid and startling dreams. Do you want me to tell you about them?"

"No. We have to work now, for a while at least. You can tell me about them later if you like."

"Why do I have to work, Sally? What is it all for?"

"Everyone should learn something, Snow. You know that. It disciplines your mind."

"What use is that?"

"You don't want to go through life ignorant of everything, do you?"

"It wouldn't bother me, particularly. I can see why Sam has to learn things. He has to grow up and get a job. But I don't. I'll never have to work or do anything, so why go to all this trouble?"

"How are you going to live when you grow up?"

"I'll marry somebody and live with him and look after his house and his children. I know how to do that already."

"Yes. But he might like you to be able to talk to him and take an interest in his work, mightn't he?"

"Mamma never talks to Pappa about his work."

"I'm sure she does."

"She doesn't. He is interested in Irish and how people make bread and sow potatoes and cut turf and she thinks all that is a frightful bore."

"But your mother is interested in many things herself. She has read a lot of books."

"She didn't have to study when she was little, like me."

"I'm sure she did." Sally was getting exhausted by this argument, which was played out in the nursery almost every day. She walked to the window.

From here the park was a fluff of soft round green cushions. All the trees were in leaf. The flowerbeds were splashes of bright June colours – red geraniums, deep blue delphiniums, lupins in pinks and yellows. Sally did not know the names for most of them. The gardener was walking around, waving his stick at people who he thought were breaking one of the many rules of the park. Already some children were down there, playing, while those who looked after them sat on the park benches and read their newspapers.

Snow observed Sally's face.

"Let's go down," she said. "It is a shame to waste such a lovely day cooped up in here learning grammar. Especially since I'm not going to learn anything anyway."

Sally turned on her angrily.

"No!" she said. "You have to spend three hours working every morning. I can't have any more of this."

She spoke so angrily that she shocked herself. Snow looked at her in astonishment, and began to read her book.

Sally sat in the wicker chair that stood at the side of the window and stared at the park and the street outside. She saw the various delivery boys cycling along with their baskets full of parcels, calling at the various houses. She saw the tram, slowly slipping along in its grooves to the terminus just around the corner. She saw the postman coming up the path and walking down again.

"Excuse me for one moment," she said. "I'm going to see if there is a letter."

She hardly ever got letters. But it was over a week since she had written to Katie, and she thought there was a chance that a reply might have come.

She was right.

There on the floor of the hall was a little heap of letters, mostly addressed to Mrs Erikson. But there was one for Sally Gallagher.

She ran back upstairs.

Snow had to comment.

"You got a letter! You never get letters! Who is it from?"

"I think it's from my sister," said Sally, tearing open the letter.

But it wasn't.

"Dear Sally," the letter went. "Thomas and I enjoyed meeting you last night and would like to ask you to meet us again on Friday. We will be at the tram terminus in the park at half past seven, and will give you a lesson in bicycling.

I hope you can come."

The letter was from Ethel.

Normally Sally would have been delighted to receive such a letter but she was disappointed.

Don't be stupid, she said to herself. Why would Katie write now? She hasn't written for months.

But she felt upset nevertheless and decided to write another note to Katie, to impress upon her the need to contact her.

"It's not from my sister," she said absently, forgetting that she had asked Snow to concentrate on her work. "It's an invitation to learn to cycle. Ethel . . . somebody called Ethel . . . will show me how."

"You'll have to ask us for permission," said Snow, cheekily. "Maybe Mamma won't want you to learn to cycle. She thinks it's dangerous."

"I'm free on Friday evenings," said Sally, annoyed. "And I want to learn. It is up to me."

"Nothing is really up to you, Sally, is it?"

"Go on reading, Snow. You are just trying to distract me."

Sally thought she would like to pick Snow up and shake her very hard, but she resisted the temptation. In theory, the younger girl was right. But in practice, Sally knew she had plenty of freedom and little to complain about.

Seven

Sally on Wheels

On Friday evening, Sally made her way to the tram terminus. She had asked Mrs Erikson if she could go out, to learn to cycle, and Mrs Erikson said yes, as she usually did to any reasonable request.

It had been a fine sunny day, and the sun was still shining at half past seven. Sally walked slowly along under the thick trees, savouring the greenish light and the fresh, summery smells.

The tram terminus was in a circular green at the top of Palmerston Park. Behind it was the park, and in front the long elegant road, wide as a boulevard, stretched for half a mile in the distance. Neither Ethel nor Thomas were at the tramstop when she arrived. She sat on a park bench conveniently placed near it and waited, keeping an eye on the road.

Soon she saw two black spots moving up the road. Gradually they materialised into the shapes of Ethel and Thomas, cycling along. Thomas was wheeling a spare bicycle alongside his own.

"Good evening to you!" sang Ethel gaily, when she was within shouting distance. "You havn't been waiting long, I hope?"

"Oh no," said Sally. "Just a minute or two."

She stared admiringly at Ethel's outfit: she was dressed in a dark green jacket and dark green cycling skirt, with a matching hat. Sally wondered how she managed to keep the hat on while cycling, but women did this all the time.

"How are you?" said Thomas, who was dressed in tweed knickerbockers. He jumped from his bike and leaned it against the bench. "Fighting fit?"

"Yes, thank you."

"You'll need to be!" laughed Ethel. "This one is for you! It belongs to my mother but she seldom uses it."

"I can't imagine how you do it," said Sally. "It looks like magic. How can you balance on two thin wheels?"

"I don't know," said Ethel. "It looks like something in a circus, I know. But it seems to just happen."

"It's to do with the laws of motion," said Thomas learnedly.

'Oh really?" said Ethel. "What laws would that be now?"

"Well . . . you know. Some law that says if you keep moving on two thin wheels you won't fall off but if you stop you will."

"That's most enlightening, Thomas," said Ethel. "I'm sure it makes Sally feel much more confident."

"I'd like to try it anyhow," said Sally.

"Of course," said Ethel. "Go ahead."

Sally took the bicycle handlebars in her hands and sat on the saddle.

The bicycle toppled over immediately and she tumbled down onto the ground.

"I don't seem to be able to do it!" she cried. "It just won't stay upright for long enough!"

"You have to . . . you have to sort of get up and onto the saddle and start pedalling all at the same time," said Ethel.

"But how can I do that?" protested Sally. "I mean I can't

do three different difficult things all at exactly the same time."

"Well, maybe not exactly . . . you just have to get moving quickly."

"Show me how!" said Sally.

Both Thomas and Ethel hopped up on their bicycles and flew off down the road at high speed. Sally watched them with a mixture of admiration and disbelief. Cycling looked as easy as walking. And it was as easy as walking, if the huge numbers of people cycling around Dublin were anything to go on.

Well, people had to learn to walk. It's just that it happens when you are so young that you can't remember how you did it, or if it seemed difficult at the time or not.

"That's how it's done!" said Thomas. He and Ethel dismounted once again and laughed kindly at Sally.

"I'll just have to keep trying, I suppose!" she said, sounding more optimistic than she felt. She looked at the bicycle, a heavy black iron machine. It was beginning to look like an enemy to her.

"I know what we can do!" said Thomas. "I'll hold the bike steady while you get on, and then when you're settled you can set off in your own good time!"

"Yes!" said Sally. "That's a good idea."

She gave the bicycle a firm no-nonsense look. Thomas held it at the back and Ethel held it at the front. Sally clambered up onto the saddle, which felt much higher up than it looked, and gripped the handle bars.

"Great!" said Ethel. "You're on! All you have to do now is start pedalling."

She let go.

Sally screamed.

"Please don't let go! Don't let go yet."

"All right," said Ethel. "But I have to let go sometime."

"I'll say when."

"I can hold on even when you start moving," said Thomas, "if that makes you feel more secure."

"It does," said Sally. "It makes me feel much more secure. Please do that."

"All right," said Ethel, still gripping the bicycle from the front. "I'm at your command. Tell me when the moment is ripe."

Sally sat on the bicycle, which wobbled ferociously even though it was gripped fore and aft.

"You will have to start sometime," said Ethel. "But take your time, don't worry about us! It's amusing, standing here holding a bicycle up. I could do it all day!"

"Oh God," said Sally. "All right. All right. Let go now Ethel."

Ethel let go.

The bicycle wobbled precariously and Sally's hat fell off.

"Don't worry about that!" said Ethel. "Start moving!"

Sally started to push the pedals.

The bicycle edged forward.

"Keep holding on Thomas," she said.

"Don't worry. I won't let go," he said. "You can depend on me."

"Go a bit faster," said Ethel, picking up Sally's hat. "Just a bit faster. Thomas will enjoy running along behind!"

Sally increased her speed.

She pushed the pedals and moved a few yards along the road.

"Just a little faster!" said Thomas. "I can *walk* faster than this!"

She pedalled harder. The bicycle moved faster.

She began to pedal quite quickly. Push push push push. She could feel the machine steadying itself, moving firmly, like an arrow – a *slow* arrow – through the air. She pedalled a little faster.

"Are you still there?" she asked.

"Yes!" shouted Thomas.

She went faster.

"I'm doing it," she said. "I'm doing it!"

Then she remembered that she wasn't really doing it. Thomas was holding on.

"Getting tired, Thomas?" Sally shouted.

"No," said Thomas. His voice sounded far away. Sally glanced over her shoulder. Thomas was not behind her. She could see him and Ethel, several yards away, jumping up and down and cheering.

Sally turned back around and began to wobble precariously. Before she knew what was happening, she tumbled off the bike.

"How could you do that to me?" she said, wheeling it back to them. She was so alarmed that she forgot to be shy. "I could have . . . been killed or anything."

"It's not so easy to get killed falling off a slowly moving bicycle," said Thomas, "unless somebody runs into you."

"Still, it was . . . unkind."

"No it wasn't," said Thomas. "It was not unkind, because now you can ride that bicycle. Just try it on your own."

"I feel so . . . tired . . . "

"Up you go!" said Ethel.

Sally got up. After a shaky start, she cycled about a hundred yards down the road to the corner and then came back again.

"You see. It's as easy as anything," said Ethel.

"It is, isn't it, when you know how. And when you don't it seems so impossible!"

"Yes. It's true. It's like learning to swim. First you can't do it at all, and then you can do it. There's no in between. It's not like French or Latin or anything."

"Or Irish," said Sally.

"Well, Irish probably wasn't hard for you, since it's your first language!"

"No, of course not. But it seems to be hard for Snow."

"Snow?" said Thomas. "What sort of a creature is Snow? Sounds like a cat or a dog or something."

"Snow is my pupil," said Sally, slowly. Her face reddened in spite of herself."

"Your what?" Ethel exclaimed.

"My pupil. I work as a governess," Sally was panting, from the exertion of cycling and from nerves. Ethel and Thomas would presumably say goodbye to her now, and she would never see them again. And just as well too!

"A sort of governess, for the Eriksons. My pupil is Snow Erikson. They called her that because Professor Erikson misses the snow. At least that's what Biddy says."

"And who is Biddy?" Ethel was looking at her curiously. Perhaps she had never talked to a governess before . . .

"The maid in the house."

"Ah!" Thomas and Ethel exchanged a quick glance. Then Ethel said quickly

"Indeed, I know the Eriksons. I didn't realise . . . " her voice trailed off and she blushed over her freckled face. Then she continued quickly. "That Snow Erikson is a mischief maker. She's always caused trouble, since she was so high. The Eriksons have had about ten governesses."

"Yes, I know," said Sally. "But I have lasted a good while."

"You must be a genius," Ethel exclaimed. "Snow . . . " Words failed her. She began to get back up on her bicycle.

"Her brother is nice, though. Sam. He's not like Snow at all."

"I thought he was away in England?" Ethel's face flushed.

"He's at home now," said Sally. "He came home early for the summer holidays."

"Oh!" said Ethel. "Good. Tell him I was asking for him!"

Sally smiled at her. Apparently she was not concerned that Sally was a governess, little better than a housemaid, even though she, Ethel, was – obviously, it seemed to Sally – a gentleman's daughter, and a young lady of leisure.

"Let's have one last spin around the park before we go," Thomas suggested.

"You're not supposed to," said Sally. "There are signs. 'No cyclists'."

"We know that," said Ethel. "But we love to cycle along the paths, under the big trees. It's heavenly. Rules were made to be broken, you know"

They went up to the big gate. It was locked.

"He's already closed the park," said Sally, deeply relieved. "I heard the keeper going around ringing his bell just before you came."

But they were not going to give up so easily.

"We won't let a little thing like that stop us!" said Thomas. "Follow me!"

They cycled slowly – because of Sally – around to the back of the park. There the railings stopped and were replaced by a high stone wall. Thomas led them along this grey, forbidding wall to a small wooden door. The door was locked with a chain from which a big iron padlock dangled. It looked very secure to Sally.

Thomas got off his bicycle and went to the door. He took a nail from his pocket and inserted it in the padlock keyhole. He fiddled it around for a few seconds. Miraculously the padlock opened! He pulled back the chain and pushed open the door.

"Entrez!" he said, *"S'il vous plaît!"*

"That means come on in," said Ethel. She cycled through the doorway. Sally followed her, a little timidly.

"How does he do that?" she asked. She was a bit alarmed by Thomas's ability to pick locks.

"I don't know," said Ethel. "It's just one of his many little talents. Picking locks. He could be a professional thief if he wanted to."

Thomas followed them into the park and closed the door behind him.

"Do you ever worry about being locked in?" asked Sally, who was still feeling very worried.

"No," said Thomas. "I know I can get out. We could climb over the railings anyway, if all else failed."

"But we won't need to do that," said Ethel. "We never do."

"Do you do this often?"'

"Yes. Every week, at least once. Let's go!"

They cycled along the darkening paths, under the spreading trees. The park was twilit, dim, quiet as a mountain valley. They cycled past the sleepy flowerbeds, under a wooden arbour hung with clematis and honeysuckle, into a small garden filled with white marble statues of half naked men and women which Sally had not seen before, and which looked eerie in the half light.

"It's great, isn't it?" said Ethel. "Doesn't it feel different from during the day?"

"Yes, completely different," said Sally. "I've never been in a place which felt like this . . . "

It felt more silent and ghostly than the loneliest glens in Donegal. And why was that, she wondered? Maybe it was because the park was, during the day, such a busy populated place, with children playing and old people strolling and ducks being fed and dogs being called to. And there was always the gardener, in his black suit, moving around, pottering among the flower beds or keeping an eye on the boys sailing boats on the pond.

55

Sally looked again at the statue. There was one of a woman with curly hair, like snakes, twining around her head. She didn't have any arms; they had been broken off just above the elbow. But she had the legs and feet of a horse.

Sally stared at the strange white figure.

There was something captivating about her . . . she seemed to be about to move. She seemed to be about to come alive.

"It's a bit strange," said Sally, turning to Ethel.

But Ethel had disappeared. And so had Thomas.

"Ethel!" Sally whispered. "Where are you?"

There was no reply.

Sally looked again at the white statue.

Slowly, a smile spread across its stony face.

Eight

The Statue

Sally stood, frozen with terror, in the shadowy, twilit garden.

"Ethel!" she screamed. "Thomas! Where are you?"

There was no reply. She heard birds twittering, and small scurrying sounds – squirrels and hedgehogs, mice and birds, out on their nightly hunting.

Sally, who had been standing straddling the bicycle, threw the machine on the ground and dashed away from the walled garden as fast as she could.

She ran and ran. She ran through the clematis arbour and along the chestnut path. She ran down to the pond. It shimmered, still and black as the midnight sky, under the shuddering, shivering trees. "Ethel!" she screamed. "Thomas!"

A bat swooped out of the shadows and sped past her. It moved so fast that it had vanished into the twilight long before she realised what it was. But she had felt a brush of air as the tiny creature swished past, and it had added to her panic.

Where could Thomas and Ethel have gone? How could they have disappeared so quickly?

How could they have done this to her?

She looked over her shoulder. The white statue was no longer to be seen.

She breathed more easily, and stood for a few second's rest, planning to run back to the door in the wall and see if she could find Thomas and Ethel there. While she stood she continued to keep an eye on the area behind her.

There was no sign of a white figure.

But a black one loomed out of the shadows. Sally could hear the crunch of boots on gravel.

The keeper of the park.

He was waving his stick in the air, and walking hurriedly towards the pond.

Sally picked up her skirts and ran again.

It was not far to the wooden door. She ran as fast as she could, her heart in her mouth, her blood pumping. Never in her life had she run as fast as this.

The door loomed ahead. It looked closed and unfriendly, hostile as a door to a dungeon.

She ran up against it without even stopping, expecting it to block her way. And then the keeper – what would he do? What was the penalty for breaking and entering a public park? Probably several weeks in prison.

The door opened easily and she toppled out into the shadowy lane.

She pulled the door closed behind her and ran back towards the railings.

Just around the corner, where the wall gave way to railings, Ethel and Thomas were standing, hidden behind a huge sycamore tree.

"Sh!" said Ethel. "We waited for you."

"Let's get out of here!" said Thomas. "Where is your bike?"

"I left it behind!" said Sally.

"Oh dear!" said Ethel. "What am . . . "

"Never mind that now," said Thomas. "We have to get away before he catches us. Let's go down that road there."

They all walked very quickly, Thomas and Ethel pushing their bikes, away from the park, down a road lined with big houses. Thomas led them onto another road and then turned a corner.

"Ethel," he said. "Shelter!"

"Yes, yes, come in," said Ethel. "I live here," she explained to Sally. "In that house there."

She pointed to a house which was much bigger and grander than the Eriksons. It was also much more exotic, since the person who had designed it had modelled it on a fairytale castle. The house had turrets, battlements, and pointed windows with black leaded panes in them.

"Don't worry about it," said Ethel. "It looks like Dracula's castle on the outside, but inside it is quite ordinary."

"I thought . . . " said Sally. "I saw a statue . . . it frightened me, in the dark." She did not know how to explain what happened. Thomas and Ethel would think her a terrible fool. And she hardly knew them!

"Oh? Why? Was it the keeper?" Thomas was politely amused.

"Yes," Sally mumbled. "Well, no, not just him. It was a statue . . . suddenly I saw a terrible white statue, with a horse's legs. It seemed to . . . " Words failed her.

"A centaur," said Ethel, kindly. "I know the one you mean. It looks awful."

"Yes. Suddenly it seemed to appear out of nowhere. I thought . . . it smiled at me." She shuddered. "It was terrible."

"Hm," said Ethel. "My mother would probably say that it did smile! She is a spiritualist. She believes in ghosts and the dead coming back and all that sort of thing."

"Oh," said Sally, looking at the house with even more dismay.

"Do you think she'll believe her bicycle will come back?" asked Thomas, with a laugh.

"He'll never give it to us. That old park keeper. Mother will not be pleased when she finds out."

"She needn't find out, need she?" said Thomas. "At least not immediately."

"No," said Ethel. "I won't let on. And maybe we'll manage to get it back . . . Let's go inside."

"Your mother?"

"She's not in. She's at a meeting of some kind," said Ethel hurriedly. "Perhaps a seance. We won't have to worry about an excuse tonight. Come on!"

They walked down the long gravel drive. Then Ethel led them down a flight of stone steps, partly covered with green moss, into a dark, damp area. She opened a door and they went into the basement of the house.

The kitchen was in the basement. It was a large, warm room, not unlike the kitchen at the Eriksons. There was a range and a big table, and a dresser. There were many pots, silver and copper, hanging from the walls. What was unusual about this room was that, hanging from one wall was a selection of swords and spears.

Ethel noticed Sally's interest.

"My father collects them," she said. "He has so many that they have to be hung even in the kitchen. The whole house is full of lethal weapons."

"How interesting," said Sally, feeling that this house was not in the least bit normal or safe.

"I'll show them to you sometime," said Ethel. "But let's have some cocoa now. We need it after that escapade."

"Where did you go?" asked Sally. "You were both right behind me and then the next minute you were nowhere to be seen!"

"We saw him . . . " said Ethel, looking up from the range. Sally thought it odd that there was no servant visible in such an enormous house.

"He saw us. The keeper. Old Byrne. And then we had to cycle off as fast as we could."

"He hates us. He wants to kill us with that stick of his," said Ethel.

"I thought you said nobody ever saw you getting into the park?"

"Well, nobody sees us, as a rule, I think it is true to say," said Ethel. "But old Mr Byrne knows we get in all the same. He's seen us and he can sense us."

"How?"

"Intuition," said Ethel. "There is such a thing. You know, my mother says we only ever use ten per cent of our brains. There is a whole side to our intelligence that we never make use of."

"But your mother does?"

"Ethel!" said Thomas warningly. "Why don't you just make the cocoa."

"Oh stop telling me what to do, Thomas," said Ethel. "He is such a sceptic," she turned to Sally, who was beginning to thaw out a little in the warm, dark kitchen. She was beginning to feel a bit sleepy, even.

"Thomas is what my mother calls a rationalist. Doubting Thomas. He only believes what he sees with his own two eyes."

"Well, so do I," said Sally.

"Yes," said Ethel. She took three china cups from a dresser and poured hot cocoa into them. She put them on the table. "Yes. But you have seen a marble statue smile tonight."

"Well," Sally was feeling more comfortable now, in the warmth of the kitchen. "It was probably just my imagination."

"It was twilight," said Thomas. "The light plays tricks on

61

you just at that time, before it gets dark. It's sort of like that painting technique . . . *trompe d'oeil*, you know?"

"Mm," said Sally, who did not know.

"I am quite sure that you saw the statue, and I want you to tell Mother all about it sometime. I think she's with the Rosicrucians."

"What is that?" Sally yawned. She felt more and more sleepy, and could hardly keep her eyes open or pay any attention to what was being said.

"It's a society of spiritualists, people who believe that they can talk to ghosts and the dead. They have seances. My mother uses them to talk to her mother, who died twenty-five years ago when Mother was just twenty."

"Mm," said Sally. "I'd love to talk to my father."

"Your father is dead?" asked Thomas, with kind interest.

"He was drowned at sea some years ago," said Sally.

"That is very sad," said Ethel. "Mother could help you to get in touch. Would you like to see her ouija board?"

"Don't, Sally," said Thomas. "It really is so nonsensical. They only get 'in touch' by knocking. You'd just hear your father knocking on a table. Or rather you'd hear somebody pretending to be your father knocking on a table. Do you think that would be so wonderful?"

"Well, knocking isn't the same as talking."

"If you talked to Mother you'd think differently. She talks to people on the other side all the time. She has long marvellous conversations and they give her advice on all kinds of things."

"We need advice," said Thomas. "On how to get that bike back before old Byrne sells it to someone else. But I don't think we'll get it from ghosts."

"You're going to have to work that out yourself," said Ethel. "In the meantime I want to know, what did Sally see?"

"Moving light," said Thomas.

"Why would one of those statues smile at anyone anyway?"

"I don't know;" said Sally. "What are they? I never saw anything like them before."

"They're reproductions of classical statues from Greece and Rome," Ethel explained. "Mostly they're gods – Venus and Jupiter and you know, people like that. You say the one that frightened you was a centaur . . . "

"Yes. A big woman with no arms."

"A centaur is a man with the head and trunk of a man and the feet of a horse. Are you sure it wasn't one of the others you saw? Maybe Venus? She's a woman with curly hair. Maybe it is an omen. Perhaps you are about to fall in love!"

"I don't think so," said Sally.

Thomas gave her a little smile.

"I don't really want that to happen," she said, noticing the smile and averting her eyes. "Not at the moment anyway." Sally decided to change the subject. "Do you know,"she said, "I really must be getting home. It's getting very late."

"I'll walk you home," said Thomas.

Sally and Thomas left the house by the kitchen door.

It was very dark now. The gaslamps on the street had been lit and only they glowed, throwing a yellow, shimmery puddle of light on the path just outside the gate.

Sally and Thomas left, and the gate creaked shut behind them. They began to walk down the road.

When they had gone a few yards, Sally heard footsteps behind. She turned to look.

The white statue stood, in the puddle of yellow gaslight.

Sally let out a small scream.

"What is it?" Thomas clutched her elbow.

Sally pointed.

"That's her. The statue."

It was a woman with curling ringlets falling over her shoulders, dressed all in white. Instead of a hat she had a white lace mantle on her head. Her face was white in the lamplight.

"Good night, Mrs Johnston," Thomas said.

"Oh, is that you, Thomas?" the lady spoke in a high-pitched, pretentious tone. "Goodnight!"

Nine

A Gift Bicycle

"Mrs Johnston, Ethel's mother." Thomas offered this information with a little smile.

"That woman is Ethel's mother?" Sally felt both surprised and foolish.

"Why yes," said Thomas. "I'm so sorry. I should have introduced you."

"Oh no," Sally said quickly. "It is so late . . . And she looks so strange, doesn't she?"

"Well, she's a little pale, perhaps. I wouldn't call her strange."

"She looks like that statue in the park." Sally shivered. She was glad of Thomas's company, since it was very dark, and the rustling of the trees in the cool night sounded not friendly, but threatening.

"Were you very frightened?" Thomas asked, sympathetically.

"Yes. I can't stop thinking of the statue. It had such an evil face."

"It must have been horrible."

"Well, I know it must have been my imagination, or the light, or something . . ." Or Ethel's mother, Sally was thinking. But she could not bring herself to utter such a suspicion aloud. Thomas would laugh at her and think her mad.

"We shouldn't have left you alone."

"Oh well . . . " Sally looked at him gratefully. She knew he thought the statue in the park had been a pure mirage. It surprised her that he nevertheless sympathised with her and seemed to understand how terrifying the experience was.

"Parks are strange places, at night," he said. "They change character completely, somehow."

Sally looked uneasily over the dark green railings.

"They do," she said. "Somehow this park looks much darker and stranger than any lonely mountainside or bog. I don't know why."

"Do you miss the mountains and the bog?" Thomas asked.

"You mean am I homesick? Of course, a bit," said Sally. "But not as much as you might think. I'd like to see my mother, of course, sometime," she added. "And my sister."

"Will you be able to go back on holidays?"

"I don't know," said Sally. "I'm not sure if I have any holidays. The Eriksons haven't mentioned any."

"You should ask them. I think they will let you go, for a while, if you ask. They seem particularly generous employers."

"Oh yes, they are," said Sally. "They are very exceptional. Everyone says that."

By now she was at the gate of the Eriksons' house.

"I'll see you soon again, I hope," said Thomas. He squeezed her elbow and walked off into the night. Sally stood at the gate for a minute, watching him. He walked very quickly and firmly, as he did most things. Indeed he often looked and sounded impatient, as if everything and everyone in the world moved too slowly for him. But tonight he had revealed that he could be understanding and sympathetic.

Sally went down the garden steps and let herself in at the kitchen door.

Biddy was in the kitchen, sitting by the fire, knitting.

"Hello, Biddy," said Sally. "It's a lovely night, isn't it?"

"Indeed it is," Mrs Erikson spoke from a corner of the room, taking Sally completely by surprise. "Where have you been till this hour?"

Sally stared at her in surprise. Like Mrs Johnston, she was also dressed in white tonight – a white dress with a purple and green sash. Sally had asked her for permission to be away for the evening earlier in the afternoon. Of course she had known. Why was she pretending not to?

"Oh, I thought you . . . I'm sorry, I thought you knew I was taking the night off."

"Did I?"

"I think so. I was out learning to cycle, with some people I know. Ethel Johnston."

"With Ethel? Of course, her mother is a good friend of mine. I met her tonight. Where did you meet Ethel?"

"At the Gaelic League meeting I went to with Geraldina."

"Of course, of course. But that is not what I meant. I meant, where did you meet her tonight?"

"Oh, yes. Near the park."

"Near the park?" Mrs Erikson smiled. Her face was very white tonight, as if it had been covered in chalk. Probably it is just talcum powder, Sally thought. But she shivered anyway.

"I walked through the park tonight, with Mrs Johnston, after the meeting in the Mansion House."

"Mansion House? Is that where the Rosicrucians meet?"

"It wasn't the Rosicrucians, bless you, child. It was the Irish Women's Suffrage Association. The more meetings I go to the more I despair of us ever getting the vote!"

"Oh," Sally was only half listening to what was being said. "And you went for a walk in the park? After dark?"

"It was almost dark, yes. We got locked in, as a matter of fact. The keeper had to let us out."

"That happened to me too," Sally said. "I got locked in. And," she added "Something terrible has happened."

"What's that?"

Sally wanted to bite out her tongue. Why should she tell Mrs Erikson about the bicycle?

"The bicycle I was using was stolen."

"Dublin is full of thieves. The rate of crime is getting higher every minute, it seems to me."

Suddenly Mrs Erikson's cheeks flushed, and she did not look so frightening any more.

"Yes, indeed and it is," said Biddy. "I know a woman had her nightdresses taken from the clothesline only last week, and three good sheets."

"How was your bicycle stolen?"

"Oh, I left it against a railing, near the park, and went for a walk. And when I came back it was gone."

"Of course it was if you hadn't locked it!" said Biddy. "What else do you expect? Didn't your friends tell you you can't leave a bicycle unlocked?"

"It was just for a minute," said Sally. "Ethel thinks maybe she'll get it back."

"The bicycle belonged to Ethel, did it?"

"Yes. To Ethel's mother."

"How could you have been so stupid, Sally?" Mrs Erikson spoke very sharply. "You'll have to replace it. I certainly can't do so."

Sally had not expected this reaction.

"Replace it? How could I?" she looked very worried.

"That's for you to contrive, my dear!" Mrs Erikson

yawned. "I could pay your salary directly to her, perhaps, until due recompense was made."

"That would take months!" Sally felt that she had been punched in the stomach.

"The better part of a year, I should think," Mrs Erikson yawned again. She glanced at the clock on the kitchen wall.

"I must go to bed. I am so exhausted!"

"Goodnight ma'm," said Sally and Biddy, in unison.

"Goodnight, girls," said Mrs Erikson, getting up and going to the door.

"What am I going to do now?" Sally wailed, as soon as she was out of earshot.

"About the ould bike?"

"Yes."

"I wouldn't lose any sleep over it if I was you, Sally. It'll be forgotten about in a few days."

"Do you think so?"

"Sure I know it as well as I know anything! Sure I know herself, don't I?"

"I suppose you do!"

"Indeed and I do!"

Next morning Sally was sitting, as usual, with Snow in the nursery. Snow was reading *The Merchant of Venice*, at her mother's request, and Sally was reading a novel by Katharine Tynan, one of the volumes from a huge collection of books in the household library. Sally sat by the window, to catch the best light, and from time to time she glanced across the road at the park. The keeper was there, moving about more smartly than usual, stopping to talk to people or to spear a piece of litter that had somehow managed to infiltrate his perfect park with his spiked walking stick. There was no sign of the bicycle.Suddenly the door opened and Mrs Erikson came into the room. Today she was dressed in one of her less striking outfits – a plain purple over-dress of lace, with a black silk skirt underneath, and a high lacy collar.

"Sally," she said. Sally waited for her to refer to the stolen bicycle but she did not. "I've something to show you! Follow me."

"Can I come too?" asked Snow.

"No," said Mrs Erikson. "You stay here and work. We'll be back in a short time."

But Snow closed the book anyway and followed her mother and Sally.

They went downstairs and out into the back garden.

The garden was very long and narrow, surrounded on two sides by a high wall of yellow brick. All along the green lawn flowerbeds were dug, brown circles, each one filled with rose trees. The grass was sprinkled with petals, red and white, pink and cream, and the air in the garden was spiked with a heavy perfume which was so strong in some places that it almost made you swoon if you breathed deeply.

Sally loved the garden but had seldom spent much time in it – it was Mrs Erikson's domain. She was often to be seen out here, pruning roses or gathering them, or simply sitting in a sunny spot, her eyes closed, dreaming.

At the bottom of the garden was a wild, uncultivated patch. This was hidden from view by a screen of apple trees. Mrs Erikson led Sally and Snow down the garden to this spot. She opened a small blue wooden gate and they were in the dump of the garden: here was a heap of dung, a broken cartwheel, rusty bedsprings, some tin bins full of old clothes, and the various kinds of rubbish that households accumulate but never feel like actually getting rid of completely, at least not until they have been stored away somewhere for years and years.

In one corner of the dump was a little wooden shed.

Mrs Erikson opened the door and went inside.

A few minutes later she re-emerged, dragging out a bicycle.

It was not an ordinary looking bicycle, however, with two wheels of equal size and a saddle and pair of pedals in the middle. It was something quite different, which Sally had never seen before.

"Here," said Mrs Erikson, "is my old bicycle!"

This bicycle had one very tiny wheel and one enormous one. The saddle was perched on top of the enormous wheel, several feet off the ground.

"It's a penny-farthing!" said Snow. "I didn't know you had one, Mamma!"

"Oh yes, I've had it for years. Would you like to try it, Sally?"

Sally was completely taken aback. Was Mrs Eirkson suggesting that she give this to the Johnstons? She didn't think they'd want it. Neither did she think she'd care to ride the contraption herself. It looked very dangerous, and she didn't know how on earth she could get up on it anyway.

"Well . . . " she said hesitantly.

"I'll show you!" Mrs Erikson said. "Pull over that old bathtub, please . . . !"

Sally dutifully pulled over an old tin bathtub which was lying between the shed and the wall. Several spiders and other small insects ran for cover when she moved the object which had lain untouched for such a long time.

Mrs Erikson turned the tub upside down, climbed up on it, and from there managed to mount the extraordinary looking bicycle.

"Now," she said, "I'll show you how easy it is!"

She moved off, through the little gate, wending her way in and out among the rosebushes to the far end of the garden and back again. Sally and Snow watched in admiration and amazement the big purple figure on top of the bicycle which looked as if it belonged in a circus.

"Your turn!" said Mrs Erikson, managing to get off the bicycle with a certain amount of dignity, which was a real achievement.

"Oh dear," said Sally. "I'm not sure that I can. This is not the kind of bicycle I tried yesterday."

Yesterday seemed far away.

"The design is essentially the same," said Mrs Erikson, not very truthfully. The design was the same insofar as both contraptions were bicycles, that is, machines made of two wheels, but in other essential respects the designs were completely different. And one of these was the height of the saddle from the ground.

"I know I'll fall off," said Sally.

"Falling off is half the fun of it," said Mrs Erikson. "No harm will come to you on this soft grass. Maybe you will get a thorn in your side, but nothing worse than that!"

"I think . . . you know, I might . . . " Sally most definitely did not want to get onto the penny-farthing. It looked dangerous, and also silly. Even if she did manage to cope with it, she could not imagine cyling down the road, in public, on such a contraption. It was years out of date, and she hadn't seen a single one on the streets of Dublin, where all sorts of vehicles paraded.

"Up you go!" said Mrs Erikson, in her bossiest voice.

Sally stepped onto the tub, and, with sinking heart, onto the bicycle.

Mrs Erikson held it for a moment and then shouted, "Off you go!"

And off she went, precariously wobbling, along the winding path through the rose trees.

When she got to the end of the garden she stopped and promptly fell off. She had to wheel the bicycle down the garden again.

"How do you get on if you don't have something to stand on?" she asked.

"The answer is simple," said Mrs Erikson. "You can't. You must have something, and preferably someone, when you use this bicycle. But of course one usually does, does one not?"

"I suppose so," said Sally.

"Quite so. And now let us go back to work. You are welcome to borrow my bicycle anytime you please, Sally," Mrs Erikson put it back in the shed.

"What . . . Mrs Johnston's bicycle?" Sally could not articulate the full question.

"You can't give it to her, my dear," Mrs Erikson responded quickly. "You'll have to find some other way of recompensing her!"

"Yes," said Sally sadly, thinking that it had not been entirely her fault. Wasn't Ethel also to blame for the loss of the bicycle, and Thomas?

Sally climbed the stairs to the nursery. As soon as she entered the low-ceilinged room she collapsed onto the daybed and buried her head in its silky cushions. After a while, she became philosophical. If she had to work for half a year to pay for the bicycle, so be it. She stood up and walked over to the window. The park lay across the road, as always, its lawns and trees and flowers spread out serenely under the warm sun. The keeper was not to be seen – he was probably having his lunch in a shed somewhere, or in the garden of statues down behind the oak copse. A few small children played. It looked inviting and peaceful. Maybe she should bring Snow over for her walk and take a look?

Ten

Doubts

Sally and Snow had gone to the park and Sally had searched for the bicycle, but to no avail. Either it had been removed from the park, or the keeper had hidden it very well.

That evening, in her bedroom, Sally examined the advertisements for jobs in the newspaper, half idly and half seriously.

"Wanted. An Industrious, tidy, tall Girl, used to plain cooking. A little washing. Two in family. £6 per year. Protestant girl preferred."

Sally wasn't Protestant and £6 wasn't enough. Mrs Erikson gave her £10.

"Humble Little Girl wanted to help with housework. Must be clean, honest and well-recommended. Wages 5 shillings a month. Apply before 11 o'clock."

That was not for Sally, either.

"Smart Country Girl. Must understand children, sew and darn. Apply to Freeman Agency."

Smart country girl sounded better. But no wages were mentioned. Sally took a note of the address, and wrote a little note, asking for details. She stuck it in the pocket of her apron, intending to post it when she had an opportunity.

But would she really want to leave the Eriksons? They were particularly good employers. They paid her well, and her working conditions were easy. What other servant, or governess, went to the theatre with her mistress, or had two or three nights off a week, without any fuss or bother? None, according to Biddy, in Dublin or anywhere in Ireland. Most of them had a half-day free once a week, and all the work piled up waiting for them when they got home after that.

Even if she got another job the problem of the bicycle would follow her.

Sally sighed, and looked around her room. It was a narrow room and quite small, probably a box room, simply furnished with a small white bed, one chest of drawers with a mirror on top, a chair and a small, old table. The walls were papered with pink and white striped paper, however, and there was an old rusty coloured rug on the floor beside the bed. It was very simple and plain, but Sally had grown fond of it. Besides, Biddy had pointed out to her, on her very first day, that it was much better than the kind of room governesses or servants were usually given.

"Why? What sort of room would that be?" Sally had asked.

"I've seen some that would put the heart crossways in you! Little cupboards at the back of kitchens, without windows or a stick in them. Attics full of rats and mice, with holes in the roof."

"This is quite nice," said Sally, politely.

"This is more than quite nice, my lady. This is the best. Count your blessings. I do."

"Yes."

Sally blew out the candle and slid into bed, but it was a long time before she could sleep. Her body was exhausted but her mind could not stop working. The grinning statue, the lost bicycle, the nasty looking advertisements in the newspaper, with their demands for tall girls or Protestant girls or humble girls who could turn their hand to anything, ran in and out of her head like dozens of black rabbits, diving into a burrow one after the other. As soon as one dark thought left her head it was succeeded by another. One minute she was agonizing over her sister Katie. Why didn't she ever write? The next thing she saw herself being arrested by a big policeman, for stealing Ethel's mother's bicycle, or for entering the park without permission. The white statue grinned at her, the black-clad keeper chased her waving his big stick in the air. Her boyfriend of long ago, Manus, slammed a door in her face. Snow screamed at her "I will not learn anything!"

Hours after she had tucked herself under her white quilt, she fell asleep. It seemed no time at all before she was hearing Biddy's loud hammering on the door, telling her to get up. And she was pulling herself reluctantly from her bed, which had become warm and welcoming only minutes before she had to leave it.

"Time to get up for Mass," said Biddy.

"Is it really Sunday already?"

"Yes. I'm going to catch ten o'clock. Will you go to nine o clock?"

"Yes, of course," said Sally.

They always had to go to Mass at different times, so that one of them would be in the house in case any work needed to be done.

Sally put on her Sunday dress – a lilac and white striped cotton, which she loved, although it was far from fashionable – and straw hat, and set off alone to the church, as she did every Sunday. Usually she loved this walk through the deserted neighbourhood. The streets which were so busy all the rest of the time looked so clean and peaceful on a sunny Sunday morning, like a child who has just had a bath after a long, very active day, and is now stretched out sleepily ready to fall asleep. Rathmines looked dreamy, with only a few people walking on the pavement, one horse and car trotting along the road. Not a single tram. Even though she was tired, with that edgy, nervous morning tiredness you get when you haven't slept properly, Sally felt the peacefulness of the surroundings seeping into her. The sun shone brightly, dancing merrily over everything. It was not possible to worry about evil things, to imagine that the worst was about to happen, on such a morning.

The church bells rang out over the streets. Their loud clang boomed, throbbing over the cobblestones, filling the bricks and the stones and Sally's body with their rhythms. She could feel the ringing deep inside her, in her bones, and she found herself swinging along, keeping time with the jingle jangle.

"Good morning to you!"

The cheerful tones of Geraldina overtook her, and Geraldina was at her side.

"Good morning," said Sally.

"Going to church?"

"Yes, I am."

"I am too. To the other one, of course. But I am so glad to have met you. Why haven't you been at rehearsals?"

"Rehearsals?"

"For the play. The play the Gaelic League is doing."

"Oh dear. I'm sorry."

"We met last night, and everyone was disappointed that you were not there. They really feel you should play the part of Maire."

"I'm sorry. I didn't forget, but I wasn't sure if I was really supposed to go or not."

"Of course you are. Everyone is depending on you."

"I'll try, Geraldina. It isn't easy to do everything. I'm not sure how much free time I am supposed to have."

"As much as you can get. You are a governess, Sally, not a servant maid. Don't forget that! You have different rights and privileges now."

"I suppose so. Nothing is said, specifically."

"No, it never is. But don't talk too much to Biddy, for instance. Don't regard yourself as being on the same level as her."

"Well . . . Biddy is my friend."

"Of course, of course. I mean you should not think that because Biddy gets one afternoon off a week that you should get the same. That's all I mean. And also . . . if you associate too much with her people will begin to think you are to be treated like her. "

"Even Violet?"

"Especially Violet. Everyone is the same when it comes to this sort of thing. Believe me. I've been a governess myself, remember. You have to make it clear that you are a cut above a servant. If you don't, you'll be treated like one."

"I suppose so."

"Be sure of it. And you know what sort of life they have?"

"Well, it's not much of a life."

"It's no life at all. No freedom, no holidays, very little money. Be careful! Come to the rehearsals."

"All right," said Sally. "I will."

When she went home after Mass Biddy told her that Mrs Erikson was in bed, with a headache, while Sam and Professor Erikson had gone out.

"I've put her to bed and given her some hot milk," said Biddy. "Divil a haporth is the matter with her. But she needs a rest. Her nerves do be at her. She's looking for the doctor. I'll call in on him on me way home from Mass."

"Will you?" said Sally, thoughtfully. "I'll look after Snow."

Snow was in the garden, trying to ride the penny-farthing bicycle.

"I just can't get up on it," she said. "It's not fair."

"I can't get up on it very easily either," said Sally. "Did you never have a bicycle of your own?"

"I had one of those three wheelers," said Snow, "when I was younger. But it looks so stupid, I couldn't use it now."

"Where is it?" Sally asked.

"I don't know. Maybe in that shed where this one was."

"Let's have a look."

They went down the garden to the wilderness at the end, and looked in the old shed. It was so piled with rubbish of all kinds that it was almost impossible to see what was in it. But after poking around for a quarter of an hour amongst ancient wheelbarrows and buckets with holes in them and paint cans with half an inch of rock hard paint in the bottom they found it, buried under a mattress with the ticking falling out. It took a lot of effort to remove the heavy, damp mattress. Eventually they did and, with bits of straw sticking out of their hair and clothes, came out of the shed pulling a rusty blue tricyle.

"It's still big enough for you," said Sally. "Try it!"

Snow got on the tricycle, which was big enough for a small adult, and biked down the garden path.

"It's lovely," said Sally. "Later I think we can go out for a cycle somewhere. Wouldn't you like that?"

"Yes I would," said Snow. "Can't we go now?"

"No, not until Biddy comes back. Your mother is not well. Why don't you go and put on some clothes which will be suitable for cycling, or for tricycling? Something loose and warm."

"Where will we go?" asked Snow.

"It's a surprise," said Sally, who did not know herself.

Biddy came back at noon, with the doctor in tow. He examined Mrs Erikson and had a chat with her. He prescribed sleep and rest and gave Biddy a prescription for "something which will soothe her." Not long after the doctor's visit, Sally and Snow left.

"Stay away as along as you like!" said Biddy. "I'm grand here on me own."

Sally knew that Biddy was enjoying a chance to be alone in the house, with no one to bother her much, since Mrs Erikson was asleep, thanks to the doctor's medicine. She decided to go on a good long cycle.

"We're not just going to the park, are we?" Snow asked.

"Oh no," said Sally. "I'd like to be much more adventurous than that."

"So where will we go then?"

"First I'm going to call on Ethel. You know Ethel Johnston?"

"Yes."

"She might like to come with us."

Ethel was at home, having lunch with her parents. A servant girl asked Sally and Snow to wait in the hall. They sat on a shiny, carved wooden sofa in a high-ceilinged room, but did not have long to wait. Within seconds Ethel came out from one of the rooms off the hall.

"How good of you to call!"

"How are you?" said Sally. "I wanted to talk to you."

"Yes?" Ethel looked surprised.

"Privately," Sally indicated Snow. Ethel opened the door of the small study.

"Snow, we'll be back in a few minutes," Sally said. "Just wait here, will you?"

"Don't be long!" said Snow. "I thought we were going cycling!"

Ethel and Sally went into the dark study. It was lined with books from floor to ceiling. Sally glanced at them, thinking it would be interesting to have time to look at the titles. But she came straight to the point.

"It's about your mother's bicycle."

"Oh yes. Have you found it?"

"No. And I wondered . . . how could I . . . recompense her?"

"Recompense her? Why should you do that?"

"Well, it is a valuable thing, a bicycle."

"Yes, but it wasn't your fault. Besides, my mother doesn't even know about it yet. Don't worry about it at all. If she ever notices it's missing, I'll tell her it was stolen from me."

"But . . ."

"I am quite sure it's in the park. Thomas will go there some night and take it back."

Sally could hardly believe her ears. The problem of the bicycle had weighed so heavily on her, and now it seemed to be a matter of no importance.

"I'm afraid I told Mrs Erikson about it." She wished more than ever that she had not.

"Mm. That's a pity. But it doesn't matter anyway. She's so scatterbrained she'll never remember."

"She gave me her old penny-farthing."

"Are you going out on it?"

"I was going try it. Snow has her bicycle too."

"I'd love to go out with you," said Ethel. "It's such a lovely afternoon. But I think Thomas is going to call around in a little while, though, so perhaps he could come too. Can you wait?"

Sally called Snow from the hall and asked her if she'd mind waiting.

"No," said Snow. "Can I go out to the garden?"

"Of course," said Ethel. She rang a bell which stood on the hall table. The girl who had let Sally and Snow in came running.

"Mary, can you bring this young lady out to the back garden please," said Ethel. "That will be all."

"Perhaps I should wait in the garden too," said Sally. She had known Ethel lived in a big house, since she had visited it already, but it seemed bigger and more imposing now than it had a few nights earlier. She began to think she had made a mistake, visiting somebody like Ethel casually like this. Ethel sounded so imperious when she ordered the servant girl about and it was not so long since Sally had been a servant girl herself. Just in time she thought of what Geraldina Bannister had said to her.

"You can if you like," said Ethel. "Or you can wait here, just as it pleases you. I must go in and finish lunch, and Thomas will call in less than half an hour."

Sally decided to go out to the garden, too, and Ethel rang for the maid once again.

Ethel's garden was bigger than the Erikson's, and a different shape. It surrounded the house rather than being a patch added on behind. It was not so carefully tended and had a wild look to it. There were few flowebeds. Instead, there were many big trees and a lot of shrubbery. Snow had disappeared into some of this when Sally came into the garden.

She walked around for a while and found a small fishpond. The pond was built of old, greenish stone, and in it four or five goldfish swam round and round. A tiny fountain, a jet of water spraying out of a round naked boy with a fat face, played. There was a garden seat near the fountain and Sally sat there and turned her face to the sun.

It was quite warm. The sun was at its highest. Sally closed her eyes and turned her face to the sun. It was lovely to feel its warm rays heating her skin. She listened to the softly playing water, tinkling over the stones like piano music. In a little while she nodded off to sleep.

"Sally! Sally! Wake up!"

A soft voice was calling to her and someone was shaking her shoulder.

Sally stirred. For a minute she thought she was at home in bed, and that her mother was calling her. She thought she was back in Donegal, a little girl, getting up to go to school. She did not want to open her eyes.

"Sally!"

The voice was not her mother's. She remembered that she was on a garden bench, waiting for Ethel.

"I nodded off there," said Sally. "I didn't sleep well."

"That's all right. We can go now."

The garden swam into focus. A white woman stood over her, her face, her dress, her veil, all white. Beside her stood Thomas and Ethel.

"My mother," said Ethel. "Mother, this is Sally."

"How do you do, Sally?" said the white woman, in the high-pitched tone that Sally recognised. She extended a long, thin hand.

"How do you do?" said Sally faintly, touching the hand and shaking it very slightly.

"Mother, Sally is the girl I was telling you about. You know – who saw the smiling statue."

"Ah yes," Mrs Johnston smiled. Her teeth were uneven, whiter than most people's, but the canines were unusually long and yellow. She had a cat-like look. "Fascinating! I'm quite sure it was a spirit, you know," she stared at Sally. Sally felt cold, even though the sun was beaming warmly down on her.

"Yes. A woman was murdered in that park, many years ago. A young woman from Ranelagh, one Christmas Eve. Her body was found, mutilated, under a heap of dead leaves in the park."

Sally thought of the gardener. She could imagine him, raking the leaves into heaps. She could imagine him finding a body in one of his mountains of raked up leaves.

"And you think," began Sally timidly. "You think that she – she still haunts the park?"

"I do not think anything of the kind. I am not given to thinking things, at all," Mrs Johnston tossed her white veiled head. "I know she haunts the park. She has been seen dozens of times. The white lady of the Park. That is what you saw."

"Ah," said Sally, "I see."

"As it happens, I was in the neighbourhood of the park myself that night," said Mrs Johnston.

"And did you notice anything strange, Mother?" Ethel spoke in polite, sceptical tones.

"Well, nothing stranger than myself, I'm sorry to say, on this occasion!"

"Maybe that's what you saw, Sally? My mother!" said Ethel.

"I don't look like a statue, do I?" Mrs Johnston giggled. "I'm not even statuesque!"

"I don't think I saw anything," Sally felt cold inside, and wanted to change the subject. "It was probably just my imagination."

"I believe so," said Thomas, firmly.

"But my bicycle did disappear on that night, did it not?" Mrs Johnston said in a very quiet voice.

Sally, Ethel and Thomas all gasped.

"How do you know that?" Ethel was the first to find her voice.

"Mr Byrne, the keeper, called around with it to me this morning."

"Good," said Ethel. She exchanged a glance with Sally. "We're off, then, Mother. I suppose you would not care to join us?"

"No, thank you, my dear. I've some friends calling for afternoon tea."

"Alive or dead?" asked Ethel, as she led the way from the garden.

Eleven

On your Bike

Sally, Snow, Thomas and Ethel cycled and tricyled over the sunny roads and avenues of south Dublin, as far as Sandymount Strand.

"Usually we go much farther than this," said Thomas. "But with your machines it wouldn't be possible."

He nodded at Sally's penny-farthing and Snow's tricycle.

"We look a bit like a circus act, don't we?"

"Well, that's what the Sunday afternoon strollers seem to think!"

Everywhere along the route the foursome had been the object of amused attention. The streets were no longer deserted. Half the citizens of Dublin were out walking or cycling, enjoying the warm sunshine. The women were dressed in white or pink or pale blue muslin dresses, and carried gaily-coloured parasols to keep the sun off their skin. The children wore white smocks, or blue sailor suits.

Sandymount Strand was crowded. There were several hundred people on it. Most were going for walks, walking out to the edge of the sea on the wide, shallow stretches of sand. Some were paddling at the edge of the sea, the men with their trousers rolled up to their knees, the women with their volumnous skirts held up in bunches in front of them. A few men swam, and one woman bathed: she was dressed in a navy blue sailor dress, down to her knees, and held onto a rope, the other end of which was held by a woman standing at the edge of the waves.

"Why is she holding that rope?" Sally asked.

"In case she drowns," laughed Thomas.

The woman was standing in about one foot of water.

"Bathing is a risky undertaking, if you are a young lady," Ethel joked.

Children built sandcastles or made sand pies. Others dug for cockles and periwinkles.

Sally and her companions sat beside their bicycles, drinking lemonade which Ethel had brought in a flask in her basket. Snow played in the sand, using her hands for a spade, since she had brought none with her.

"I don't know how anyone can bear to swim here," said Thomas, looking out at the bathing men.

"I'd like to," said Ethel.

"Then why don't you?"

"Don't be silly. Not here, in front of all these people," said Ethel. "I'd have to wear a long heavy frock and hold onto a rope."

"Have you ever gone swimming?" Sally asked. She had loved to swim when she was a little girl, but hadn't for many years.

While they were discussing this, a small child came up to them and asked them for money.

"Any coppers to spare, sor?" she said.

"Run away or I'll set the police on you," said Ethel. And Sally was once again shocked to see that she had another side to her personality.

Sally looked at the little girl. She was small and thin, with a white peaky face. Her hair looked as if it had never been washed or combed. She was dressed in a brown dress that had more patches on it than anything else, and was nevertheless tattered and torn in many places. Her tiny white feet were bare. Sally had seen many children of this kind on the streets of Dublin, but usually at a distance.

"I haven't got anything to give you," Sally said as kindly as she could. "I'm sorry."

The girl walked off without any change of expression.

"You mustn't encourage people like that," said Ethel. "Those street arabs would buy and sell you. Watch your bicycle – anything that isn't tied down will walk once they're around."

"She looked so young!" said Sally.

"They start robbing when they're four or five, those children. They are a menace. The city is packed with them. I hate walking down Sackville Street, feeling them swarming all around me like flies!"

"Who are they?"

"Oh, all sorts, I imagine. Orphans, or children whose parents don't keep them under proper control."

"Where do they live?"

"I've no idea. On the streets, mainly, I think."'

"Isn't that . . . ?"

"Horrible?" Thomas finished the sentence for Sally, with a glance at Ethel.

"Well, it's not so nice to live on the streets."

"They're as hard as nails. They enjoy living on the streets. Did you see that girl's expression? Did you ever see such a look?"

"Do you think she lives on the streets?"

"I think so," said Thomas. "On the streets or in some room with about twenty other people. Haven't you ever been down in the city?"

"Not really," said Sally. It was true. Since coming to Dublin she had been to the theatre, and once or twice to Grafton Street. Most of her time was spent in the pleasant surroundings of Rathmines.

"I'll bring you sometime if you like, to Cook Street or the Coombe. Would you like to see how the other half lives?"

"She doesn't want to, I am sure," said Ethel. "She'll catch lice or something worse, and it is so upsetting to walk along those streets. They stink, and are full of horrible dogs, and the dreadful filthy children . . . ugh."

"I'd like to go," said Sally, "as soon as I can, really."

Sally was thinking that it seemed extraordinary that Ethel did not realise she was poor, not rich like her. Ethel was a nice girl but she did not find it possible to see anything outside of her own world. She had blinkers on her eyes.

"When could you go?" Thomas asked Sally.

"Well, I have a half day on Wednesday. Would that suit you?"

"It might. I'll let you know tomorrow night, if I can go to the rehearsals for the play."

"That would be nice. I think you'll find it interesting."

"I wouldn't, I'm sure," said Ethel. "I don't think it is a good idea to dwell on the unpleasant side of life. Anyone for more lemon soda and duchess biscuits?"

"I'll have more!" said Snow, appearing out of nowhere at mention of the words "lemon soda." Her hands, face and white dress were sprinkled with the greyish, dampish sand.

"You look like a street arab yourself," said Ethel. "You could be called Tatters or Flitters, instead of Snow."

"I'd liked to be called Tatters," said Snow. "It sounds like the name of a dog. I wish I had a dog."

"Why don't you?"

"Pappa doesn't like dogs."

"Get one anyway," said Ethel, who did not have a very

particular conscience. "When he is away on one of his field trips."

Sometimes Professor Erikson went away to the country, to collect information about customs and ways of life.

"Hm," said Snow, thoughtfully. "What would happen when he gets home again?"

"Then you present him with what is known as a *fait accompli*," said Thomas. "How is your Irish coming along?"

"Very well thank you," said Snow, averting her eyes from Sally's.

When they got home Mrs Erikson was up and feeling all right again. She talked to Sally and Snow about their outing, and Sally felt she could ask if she might go to the play rehearsal next week. Mrs Erikson was encouraging.

"Of course you should go," she said. "It's a great opportunity for you. Snow and I will be cosy together here, won't we dear, and Biddy is downstairs looking after everything else."

"Thank you, Mrs Erikson," said Sally, smiling. "By the way, Mrs. Johnston's bicycle has been found."

"Really? I didn't know it was lost!" said Mrs Erikson. "But I'm certainly glad it's been found."

"Yes," Sally gazed wonderingly at Mrs Erikson. "So am I."

She felt in her pocket, and fingered the letter of application for another job. She began to tear it up into tiny pieces. No job would be as unpredictable as this one with the Eriksons.

When she arrived at the room where the rehearsal was being held she recognised a number of people: Geraldina was there, as well as Thomas, and several faces which she remembered vaguely from the meeting of the Gaelic League she had attended. Geraldina greeted her enthusiastically – her Irish had improved a lot since Sally had first met her and by now she spoke it fluently, albeit in a strong south Dublin accent.

Geraldina's high spirits were shared by everyone in the room. Maybe it was because she had come from a house where the atmosphere was rather sober just at present, but to Sally it seemed that all the people here were abnormally cheerful and light-hearted. The room was full of laughs and jokes and everyone was smiling all the time, as if they were delighted just to be here, to be together and doing this thing.

"Sally!" trilled a woman with yellow hair. "I am Elinor and I am going to direct this play. We are absolutely delighted that you could come. We know you will make this play really come alive for us!

"Thank you," said Sally. "I hope I can do something for you."

"Tonight what we're going to do is read it through, once, without stopping. And next time we'll begin to work on the acting," explained Elinor.

The people around the table rustled their files of paper.

"You don't have a copy?" said Elinor. "You'll have to share. We don't have copies for everyone, I'm afraid. Tonight I'll lend you mine and then you might be able to copy it out yourself at home over the next week? That is how we have done it so far. Are you a fast writer?"

"Yes," said Sally. "I'm quite fast."

"You share it with Thomas there, then, will you?"

Sally was happy to do that.

The play was called *Casadh an tSugain* (*The Twisting of the Rope*) and had been written by the man who had addressed the last meeting of the group, Douglas Hyde, one of the men who had founded the Gaelic League. It was a short comic play, about a girl called Úna, and a poet called Tomás. Úna is engaged in the play to a boy named Séamús. But this older man, Tomás, who used to be a friend of her father, visits the house. He is a poet and comes from somewhere in Connaught, while Una and her mother live in Munster.

Tomás comes to the house one night while a dance is in progress. He has a reputation for being the sort of man who seduces young girls and makes them fall in love with him. Soon after he comes in he sits down with Úna and begins to chat her up. Úna's mother notices this and is very alarmed. She does not want her daughter's engagement broken by Tomás, who is unreliable and harum scarum, as well as being about twice Úna's age.

She plans to trick him and throw him out of her house.

She does this by getting someone to run in and shout that a carriage has been overturned at the end of the lane. The only way to pull it out is to get a big long rope. But, she says, the people of Munster do not know how to make a rope. This is a skill which only the people of Connaught possess.

The poet is unable to resist the temptation to boast. He is from Connaught, and he can make a rope.

The way ropes were made at that time was this: people got a lot of straw and twisted it in such a way that a long length of thick straw rope was created.

Tomás the poet takes some straw and begins to twist it into a rope.

Úna's mother and some of her friends feed him more and more straw.

He twists and twists, and the rope gets longer and longer.

He stands at the end of the rope, moving further and further away as it grows in length.

In the end the rope is so long that he has to go outside the door if he is to keep making it.

Úna's mother opens the door for him and lets him out with his rope.

As soon as he is outside she slams the door and bars it so he can't get back inside.

"It's a wonderful play!" beamed Elinor. "So amusing! Such rich Irish! And you read it so beautifully!"

"I think it's stupid," said Sally.

She and Thomas were walking home.

"I thought the one I saw by Yeats was good, but this is so silly."

"I think it will be better on stage than it is when you read it," said Thomas. "The plot is a bit childish, perhaps . . . "

"It's incredibly childish," said Sally, laughing. "There must be an easier way of getting rid of someone you don't like than asking them to twist you a rope!"

"It's based on some old story," said Thomas. "I think that's why he used it."

"There are much more interesting old stories than that one," said Sally. "I know a lot of them myself."

"Do you?" said Thomas. "You are so different from anyone here. You come from another world, don't you?"

"Yes, in a way," said Sally. "Have you ever been to the west of Ireland? To Donegal or anywhere like that?"

"I have been to Killarney. But I'd love to go to Donegal sometime. I'd like to go to the place you come from."

"It might surprise you," said Sally. "It's not like here and I don't think it's much like Killarney either."

They were walking under the trees near the park. Thomas put his arm on Sally's elbow and stopped walking. He looked at her gently.

"Oh Sally," he said. "You're so different from the other girls around here.'

"Am I?" said Sally. "Am I so different from the girls you know?"

"It's not that I know that many," Thomas said hurriedly. "But – it's easier to talk to you, somehow."

"Thank you," said Sally, shyly.

"Could I see you alone sometime?" he asked.

"We're alone now," Sally countered. They were almost home. She liked being with Thomas but she wasn't sure if she wanted to go out with him, which was, she knew, what he meant.

"You know quite well what I mean," Thomas said, somewhat crossly.

"Yes," Sally sighed. "It's very nice of you to ask me. But you hardly know me. And there are all kinds of things to take into account."

"Like what?" said Thomas stubbornly.

"I'm not Ethel," she said.

"I know," he replied. "Which is probably why I can talk to you."

"I mean, I am a governess. My father was a fisherman. I used to work as a hired girl. I'm not like you and Ethel."

"And what are we like? Me and Ethel?"

"You know. You're well off. You live in big houses with servants working for you. You live in the kind of house I work in. You could be my employer!"

"Wait a minute," Thomas said. "What makes you say that?"

"It's true, isn't it?"

"No, as a matter of fact, it isn't. It may be true of Ethel. But it is certainly far from the truth as far as I am concerned."

"Oh?" Sally was genuinely taken aback. She suddenly realised that Thomas had told her nothing whatsoever about himself. She had simply assumed that he was like Ethel, or Snow, or any of the middle class people of Dublin, who seemed, to her, to be rich and out of reach.

"No. I do work. I have a job, just like you."

"I thought you were a student," Sally said. "Or that you – you know . . . "

"Just idled around all day long? Taking the odd Turkish bath at the Baths in Stephen's Green? Dropping into the club?"

"Well . . . yes," said Sally, wearily.

"I am a clerk at Dockrell's, the hardware merchants. I spend my day copying invoices for timber and copper piping, things like that."

"But you seem so . . . well off. It must be a good job."

"It is a good enough job, as things go, in Dublin."

"And where do you live?"

"I have digs in Ranelagh – a room in a house in Chester Road."

"Oh yes. I know where that is," said Sally. "In one of those new little houses down there near McGuirk's Hackney Yard."

"That's it. My parents live out in Bray, in a little house down by the Dargle. You could come out and see that sometime. We could cycle out – although it is a bit far, on the penny-farthing."

"Maybe I'll get a new bicycle sometime, somehow," said Sally.

"You could borrow Ethel's"

"I don't think I want to risk that," laughed Sally.

"Oh well, perhaps you would like to risk coming to the theatre with me next Wednesday? It won't be necessary to cycle."

"I'd like that" said Sally. "If I can take some time off."

"Good," Thomas pronounced firmly. "I'll call for you at seven o'clock. Is that all right?"

"That is all right," said Sally.

Twelve

A Letter from Home

But that particular outing to the theatre was not destined to be. The very next day Sally received a letter.

Once again, she hoped it would be from her sister Katie, and once again it was not.

> Dear Sally,
>
> I am sorry to have to write this to you. I think you should come home immediately. Something terrible has happened.
>
> In haste,
>
> Your affectionate mother.

Sally sat down on the chair by the hall stand.

"What is it?" said Biddy, her round face full of concern.

"I have to go home," said Sally faintly.

"Is somebody . . . sick?"

"I don't know." Sally stared at the wall. She could hardly speak.

"Does it say something?"

"Nothing really," said Sally. "See for yourself!"

She handed Biddy the letter.

"Come down now, pet, and have a cup of tea," said Biddy.

Sally was unable to move.

"Come on, pet, it will do you good. And then we can make the arrangements."

Biddy put her arm around Sally and ushered her down the hall and downstairs into the kitchen. She seated her in her own special rocking chair beside the fire and busied herself making tea.

"It's probably nothing at all," she said. "Don't be fretting yourself until you get there now. Sometimes people make things out to be worse than they are."

"So many terrible things have been going on lately," said Sally. "Ever since I saw that white statue . . . she was a sort of omen . . . "

"What white statue is that you're talking about?"

Biddy handed Sally the hot tea and sat down beside her. Sally cradled the cup in her hands; there was comfort in its warmth.

"When I was in the park. One night a while ago I was in the park . . . and this white statue smiled at me . . . or I thought so . . ."

"A smiling statue. Glory be to God. That's very frightening all right. I'd be very frightened of the like of that. Did it talk to you?"

"No," Sally said, shortly. "It was only my imagination. But since then all these things have been going on . . . "

"Ah well, there maybe isn't any connection at all. Drink up your tea now. You'll have a journey ahead of you."

"Yes."

Sally thought despairingly of the train, the long hours of travel that separated her from home.

"The only thing to do in a case like this now is to do one

thing at a time. Don't start getting panicky or over-excited, for if you do you'll be good for nothing. You just do one thing at a time, and then it will be all right."

"That sounds like good advice, Biddy," Sally smiled at her. "Thanks for the tea. I feel a bit better now."

"I'll tell you what, pet. I'll go and tell the missus that you have to be going and I'll get the train fare from him – I suppose he hasn't paid you anything yet?"

Sally shook her head.

"And you find out when the trains go."

"How can I find that out?" said Sally.

"You can telephone the station."

"Oh, you do that, Biddy. I don't know how to use the telephone. I've never used it. Would they have a telephone in the station?"

"Oh they would, of course! Just look it up in the telephone book."

"I'd rather not, Biddy. Would you . . . ?"

"Sure of course I will, love. Just a minute now," Biddy took out the little telephone book and began to check through it.

"There we are!" she said. "The number of the station is 243. Just a minute now and I'll find out about the trains."

She began to turn the handle on the big black telephone.

The Eriksons were sympathetic with Sally.

They were all in the drawing-room. Mrs Erikson had got up now that her husband was at home, and came downstairs in a wrapper and slippers.

Mr Erikson turned to Sally.

"And now you have problems, Sally . . . "

"Yes. But I don't know what they are."

"Maybe it is something which is not too bad,"

"Maybe," replied Sally. She doubted that. She knew her mother would not write unless something really appalling had occurred.

"You know when to catch the train?"

"Yes. It leaves at nine o'clock in the morning."

"Oh Sally, can I come too?" Snow said. She was sitting on a couch dressing and undressing her doll. Ever since Sally had told her she had to go away she had been very quiet.

"I don't think you'd like it, Snow," said Sally, not knowing what she ought to say.

"I'm sure I'd love it," said Snow.

"Really, Snow, you know it is out of the question," said Mrs Erikson. "And I'm sure Sally has plenty to occupy her without you, Snow. We will have a good time. I will bring you to the zoo."

"The zoo would be no good without Sally," pouted Snow.

"She'd be company for you," Biddy said as she poured out some tea.

She put down the teapot and walked out of the room, as if she had said nothing at all.

Professor Erikson looked at his wife.

"She has a point there," he said.

"Oh yes, she has an excellent point there," said Snow. "I'd be good company for Sally and it would be a great experience for me too, seeing a new part of the world. An Irish-speaking part of the world."

Sally smiled. Snow could be clever when she wanted to be.

"But . . . what would I do without you?" Mrs Erikson looked very downcast.

"I'll be back. It would mean Sally would have to come back."

"We don't know what would await you there . . . even Sally does not know that. Disease or pestilence, starvation . . . "

"I don't think it's anything like that," said Sally. "Mother would have said, I think, if it had been."

"I think it would be good for Snow," said Professor Erikson.

"But what if Sally has to stay for a long time?"

"For more than a week or two . . . yes . . . that could be difficult."

"I could come home myself then," said Snow. "Sally could put me on a train."

"Oh, don't be absurd," said her mother. You can't go to Grafton Street by yourself. How could you come all the way from Donegal?"

"I could," said Snow. "In an emergency I could."

Thirteen

Glenbra Revisited

Two days later Sally and Snow arrived in Glenbra.

The house looked just as it always looked – white and gold, cosy and welcoming, it nestled comfortably in the shady yard, the barn and outhouses sidling up to it like chickens to a mother hen. Sally sighed happily when she saw it. She had had a long, tiring journey and she did not know what news waited for her once she stepped inside the door. But the first sight of the house filled her with a deep comfortable satisfaction. This was her place, still, her shelter from the wild uncertainties of the great world. Even though she left the house or forgot about it, it did not go away. It was always there, waiting for her, ready to embrace her.

"Home" she said to the little, tired girl at her side. "This is my home, Snow. We're here."

She knocked on the red door and pushed it in.

Her mother came rushing out, closely followed by Sally's little sister, Janey. Janey was now ten years old. She hugged Sally and danced up and down for joy.

"Janey!" said Sally, her face wreathed in smiles. "How are you? You look lovely!" Sally tried to pick her up. "I can't lift you any more, you've grown so much!"

Janey stared at Snow.

"Oh Janey, this is Snow. Snow is my pupil in Dublin."

The two ten-year-olds stood about six feet apart and eyed each other up and down, as if checking for defects.

Sally's mother clasped her and held her tightly for a minute.

"Oh Sally!" she said. "I'm so glad you could come home. Come on in!"

Sally stepped back. Her mother had grown thinner, and her usually cheerful face was pale and drawn. She was still soft and pretty, in her plain black skirt and white blouse, but there were crows' feet at the corners of her eyes and rings under them.

"This is Snow, mother," she pulled Snow over. "She is very studious, but she does not know much Irish."

Snow was gazing in wonder at these people who spoke Irish naturally, all the time. She had never heard anyone speak it like that before. She had thought Irish was a language that belonged only in books with dull grey covers and pages of tight print. Like Latin.

"Yes I do," said Snow. "I understand everything you are saying."

"Good," said Sally, raising her eyebrows in disbelief. "Come on in then."

They went into the hot kitchen. Sally breathed deeply. She loved its heat, its white walls, its red wooden bin for feed. She loved the clutter and the smells of the kitchen – the hot smell of baking bread, the dry spicy smell of barley. The sweet smell of the bunch of wild flowers her mother always placed in a jar on the windowsill. The special smells of Sally's house.

By the fire, sitting in the rocking chair, was a small black figure.

"Hello Granny," Sally said, walking over to her.

The figure turned.

Sally jumped out of her skin.

"Katie!" she cried. "What are you doing here? Why didn't you tell me she was here?"

Katie stood up. She was wrapped in a black shawl. Her face was white and her hair was duller, less fair than it had been – almost white. Her eyes had lost their shine. She walked over and Sally hugged her.

Skin and bone.

"You're so thin, Katie – " Sally hesitated. "It's lovely to see you again."

"Oh Sally, dearest Sally! I am so happy to see you too," said Katie. Tears rolled down her cheeks.

"What's the matter?" Sally looked closely at Katie's face.

Sally's mother said:

"Why don't you say hello to Granny, Sally? And then . . . "

Sally went over to the curtained recess at the back of the kitchen, where her grandmother slept and spent all her time nowadays.

She peeped in. The old woman was asleep. Her face, etched with wrinkles like a cabbage leaf, was calm and still on the white pillow. Her tiny bony hands lay on the bedcover, like skinny newborn birds.

"Hello Granny," whispered Sally. "I'm home."

She stooped and kissed the yellow face.

Granny opened her eyes slowly and looked at Sally. Then she closed them again.

"I'll talk to you later," whispered Sally. She patted the thin hands and went back to the fire.

"Granny has failed a lot," said her mother. "She sleeps most of the time. She probably didn't know who you were."

"Oh dear," said Sally. "Does she . . . know anybody?"

"Och well," said her mother. "She has good days and bad

days. One day you think it's all over and then a few days
later she's able to sit up and drink tea again."

"No more pipes for her?"

"No more pipes. She's not able for the old pipe any more
now, God help her."

Sally's mother went to the cupboard and took out a loaf
of bread and some butter.

"Sit down, Sally, and have something to drink. You must
be tired."

Sally's mother gave Snow a glass of milk and a plate of
bread and butter. Snow gobbled them up hungrily, and then,
having already examined everything there was to see in the
kitchen, asked if she could go out to explore the yard.

"Of course," said Sally, glad that Snow was pleased with
her new surroundings. "Janey can take you outside. Will
you, Janey? But stay around the house. Don't run off down
to the shore or up the mountain . . . "

"Can we go there tomorrow?" asked Snow.

"We will explore everywhere very soon," said Sally. "I
promise."

Snow backed her way to the door, gazing at the strange
room and strange faces, and then went out. Janey followed
her cautiously, not sure what to make of this new, smartly
dressed, pert little girl from Dublin. The door shut behind
them and soon their voices could be heard, rising and
falling, in the yard outside.

Sally and her mother sat at the table and had some tea
and bread and gooseberry jam. Katie stayed in her chair by
the fire.

"You must be wondering why I asked you to come
home?" her mother said.

"Of course," said Sally. "There's nothing wrong with
Packy, is there?"

She had suddenly noticed that he wasn't in the house.

"Oh devil the thing," said her mother. "Packy is the best. He's away up the hill cutting turf today. He'll be back in an hour or two for his supper."

"So," said Sally, turning towards the fire. "Katie?"

"Yes," said Katie, in a small, sad, voice. "It's me."

Sally's heart flipped over. It was years since she had seen Katie. Two years, since Katie had come home for her mother's wedding and then left again, almost immediately, for Scotland, where she had a job as a maid in some farmhouse.

"Oh Katie," she said, walking over to her and giving her a hug. "Don't worry, whatever it is. I love you."

"I'm not going to have a baby," said Katie, with a little smile.

That was what Sally had thought. Of course it was. When young girls like Katie were sad or ill, that was usually the problem. "In trouble", people called it. "So and so got into trouble."

At that time, everyone in Glenbra – everyone in Ireland – believed that being pregnant was the very worst fate that could befall a young girl who was not married. The newspapers were full of stories of girls who killed themselves because they found they were pregnant, or of girls who had been arrested because they had concealed their pregnancies and killed their babies, rather than go through with the shame of admitting that they had had one. For a girl like Katie, being pregnant would be a no-win situation. No matter what she did, she would be disgraced and punished by society – even if her own family did not disown her, as many families did.

So Sally sighed in deep relief. Katie was not going to have a baby. The worst that could befall her had not happened.

"I'm not well," said Katie. "I'm poorly."

Katie meant she had tuberculosis, a disease of the lungs for which there was no cure at that time. That is why people did not use its name. They did not like to say its name because it was so dangerous. Very few people survived it.

Sally took Katie in her arms again and hugged her for what seemed a long, long time.

The strangest thing was that she was still relieved. The thought of Katie having a fatal disease was terrible. But to Sally it seemed less terrible than the thought of her having a baby.

"Katie has gone through some hard times since you last saw her, Sally," her mother spoke gently from the table.

"Tell me what happened," said Sally.

Fourteen

Katie's Story

"When I left Glenbra the last time, two years ago, I was working in Ayrshire, for a farmer," Katie began. Sally pulled her wooden chair away from the table and closer to the fire. Her mother moved over too, to hear what Katie had to say. Katie's voice, which once had been loud and confident, was weak.

"It was a good place to be. The farmer's name was Georgie Steen, and his wife was called Maggie. I helped her in the house and the dairy, and she was very kind. They had a big farm, with thirty cows and a lot of oats and corn and potatoes, so they were well-off, but that didn't stop them being nice. They let me and all the help on the farm eat at the same table as them, for instance, and we got the same food."

"The best of food," added Sally's mother, who had heard this story before.

"Yes. There was always enough to eat at that farm – cheese and eggs for breakfast, meat and potatoes for dinner. They had a big orchard behind the house and in the autumn we had heaps of apples, and even apple tarts."

"What sort of work did you do there?"

"I did the dairy work, with two other girls, Ellie and Flora, who were from the islands, from South Uist. They spoke Gaelic, their kind of Gaelic and, can you imagine, we could understand each other very well. It was very like the way we speak ourselves, at home. That was nice, to be able to talk among ourselves when we wanted to, knowing the others couldn't understand us. We used to milk the cows, every morning. We had to get up very early. The milking started at three o'clock in the morning and finished at six. It wasn't easy, getting up at that hour in the winter, but you got used to it. When the milking was done we'd come into the kitchen and get our breakfast, and then we had to get the milk into the dairy, and pour some of it into churns, to be sold to the town, and more into pans, to separate for butter. After that I used to go back to the house to help the missus with the dinner and that."

"You had a lot to do."

"Oh yes. But it was grand. I slept in a room at the top of the house with Ellie and Flora, and we had great laughs together. And at harvest time a big crowd of girls and boys would come to work for us, for the Steens, digging the taties, and we'd have big parties at night sometimes. They'd work all day from dawn till dusk, but at night they'd sit up till all hours, singing and dancing and playing cards."

"Where did they come from?"

"They came from here, from Ireland, mostly from Donegal and some from Mayo."

"Did anyone you know come over?"

"No. I heard Neil Tinney and a crowd from down the Island were at a farm about ten miles away, but I never came across them. But it didn't matter. I had a great time anyway."

Katie paused and stared into the fire. The flames flickered

softly on the hearth, and shadows danced on the walls. It was getting dark. Sally walked over to the window and looked out. Snow and Janey were in the yard, chasing each other around the sycamore tree.

"So what happened? You didn't stay there?" Sally asked. She knew that at some stage Katie had left the farm and gone to live in the city, in Glasgow, but she had never known why she did this.

"Well," Katie smiled wanly. "It was like this. Mrs Steen, Maggie, was always very nice. She was more like another hired girl than the mistress of the house, you know. She used to laugh and talk to us, and joke about the master, and tease us about the lads in the bossie and all."

"The bossie?"

"Yes. The lads who came over from Ireland to pick the taties used to sleep in a sort of hut called the bossie, not in the big house."

"That wasn't very nice for them."

"There was no room for them anywhere else. They had bunks in the bossie, and proper blankets on them, and even an oil lamp. They had a big fire going all the time and plenty of food. It wasn't bad. It wasn't like some of the places Irish tatie hookers had to sleep in, I can tell you. In one place I heard of the barn had no beds in it at all, just heaps of dirty old straw, and they all had to sleep as best they could on that."

"Oh dear," said Sally. We've always been lucky, haven't we? Remember the Stewarts?"

"That was such a long time ago, wasn't it? But yes. There was another place not far from us where the place the hired hands were in burnt down, and they couldn't get out. They had them locked in at night and they were burnt alive."

"So your place was not like that?"

"Not at all. We used to be out in the bossie ourselves sometimes, chatting to the lads and that."

"Glory be to God," said Mrs Gallagher. "I don't like the sound of that."

"What do you expect?" asked Sally, laughing.

"It was through that, really, that I got into trouble. Not in that way!" said Katie. "But I got friendly with someone. His name was Seán and he came from Mayo. We were sort of great together, you know?"

"Yes," said Sally. "I know."

"Well, Seán came to the farm in July, two years ago, to help with the potatoes. He was very nice, much nicer than any boy I ever knew before."

Katie stopped and sighed.

Sally and her mother glanced at one another. For a minute there was silence in the warm shadowy room.

"What did he look like?" Sally asked finally.

"Oh, nice. He had fair hair and blue grey eyes, and he was taller than me, but not very tall. He was very handsome really. But the best thing about him was that he was so funny. He always saw the bright side of things and was always ready to laugh. And it wasn't such an easy life, picking potatoes. They worked from dawn till dusk, and they had to cook their own food after that. They all used to eat porridge out of one big pot in the morning, can you picture that? Everyone had their own spoon but they ate out of one big pot."

Sally thought of Palmerston Park. The big table in the kitchen, with its thick willow pattern ware. The damask table-cloths and delicate china in the dining-room. When the Eriksons ate, even when she and Biddy ate, they attacked their food with a dozen silver tools – spoons and forks and knives of several shapes.

"No," said Sally.

"Anyway," continued Katie. "I got to know Seán and we became good friends. And in September we decided we would get married. Of course I was going to write and tell you all about this, and maybe come home for the wedding and everything," said Katie. "The question was, how would we do it? Seán had planned to come back to Mayo after the harvest anyway. But we wondered if we should go back together, and live in Mayo, or stay in Scotland and try to get some money together."

"Did he have anything to get married on?"

"No," said Katie. "He hadn't a penny, except for the few pounds he'd earned for the summer's work. His father has a little farm in Erris, about ten acres, but there are ten of them and Seán comes somewhere in the middle. His brother Séamas is going to get the farm, eventually. He stays on it and helps the father."

"So . . . he wouldn't go back to Mayo?"

"No, it wasn't really practical. We decided that he would go to Glasgow when the harvest was over and try to get some work there, in the shipyards or that. We had heard that there was good money to be had in Glasgow. And I decided that I would stay on with the Steens and after a few months, when Seán had got work and a place to live, we'd get married and I would go and join him. So that is what we did."

"Very sensible," said Sally.

"Yes. Very sensible."

"Did you tell anyone about this?"

"I didn't tell Mrs Steen. She wouldn't have . . . I didn't think she would have liked it. I thought she might let me go if she knew I was planning to get married in six months. But I told Flora and Ellie. They would have guessed anyway. And when Seán left, in the middle of September, I was so sad that I needed to talk to someone about it all."

"So he went off to Glasgow?"

"Yes. He got his money, five pounds, which was a good bit, from the Steens, and he walked to Glasgow, to save the train fare. That's how all the tatie hokers got around anyway. They walked everywhere. They walked the whole way from Mayo or Donegal to Scotland, except when they were on the boat. Of course, sometimes somebody gave them a lift or that, and that made it easier. Seán thought he would get a lift part of the way and he did, in fact."

"So he wrote to you?"

"Oh yes. He had been a good scholar and he could write. We wrote to one another every week. That was great. I missed him, of course. It was always lonely at the farm when the harvest was over and all the hired hands had gone away, back to Ireland or to wherever they came from. We were all lonely for a while, and Ellie had been great with one of the lads from the islands. He didn't write to her at all. I was much luckier."

"Letters are great," Sally agreed.

"They are. So everything went on as usual. At the end of October all the harvest was finished, and the cows were in from the fields. We were settling in for the winter.

"I thought I would stay until January or February, and then go to join Seán. He wrote that he had got a job in Brown's shipyard and he was earning good money."

"Where did he live?"

"Well, he just told me he'd got lodgings and that they were all right, and of course I had the address.

"But he didn't tell me too much more about them. He seemed to think I could come and join him, and that we could get married in Glasgow. That seemed to be the best plan at that stage, rather than coming back here and spending a lot of money travelling and all. I asked him to talk to a priest and he did that, a priest at some church near where he was staying. The priest told him we should both come to him and arrange a time when we were ready. That's what we planned. That I would go to Glasgow at the beginning of February, and that we would get married as soon as we could after that. Seán thought I could get work in the city, in a shop or a factory. There was a lot of work for girls in Glasgow, he said, and work of that kind was much better paid than work as a servant girl.

"I didn't say anything to the Steens, still. I was going to tell them after Christmas, and give them some notice, but I didn't want to tell them before that. I don't know. I trusted them but not completely, I suppose. It would have been nice for me to spend Christmas with Seán but I thought I'd prefer to end my year with the MacDonalds, so they would have to pay me all my wages for the year. Anyway, Seán told me he'd only have one day off for Christmas and one for New Year. In Scotland they don't celebrate Christmas much, it's more the New Year."

"Hogmanay," said Sally, who knew things like that because she read so many books.

"That's it. Anyway we had had a good time at the Steens' the Christmas before so I knew it would be fine with them. We had good things to eat – a goose, even for us, and pheasants that Georgie shot in the woods, and roast potatoes and cake. It was lovely."

"But did that happen?"

"No. A week before Christmas Seán sent me a letter begging me to come to Glasgow. He just said that he was very lonely. His mates had left the lodgings and he had no friends. I couldn't understand it. I couldn't understand why he had been urging me to stay on the farm the week before, and now had changed his mind completely. I guessed there was something he wasn't telling me. But I decided then to leave. I went to Mrs Steen and told her I would have to go."

Fifteen

Anderson

"Did she give you your full pay?" asked Mrs Gallagher. She got up and began to make some tea.

"No," said Katie, laughing.

"So she wasn't so nice after all?"

"She was nice but maybe just a bit precise."

"Mean."

"Well. I was supposed to get ten pounds for the year's work. I had got six in June, and I would have been owed six on the first of January. But she just gave me four pounds ten, even though I was there until the twenty first of December."

"The mean ould divil," said Mrs Gallagher, pouring boiling water into the teapot with such vehemence that she nearly scalded everyone. "You were only nine days short of the month and she took nearly two months' wages off you!"

"She said she was very sorry but I hadn't given any notice, and I was putting them at a lot of inconvenience, leaving suddenly like that."

"Was that true?"

"No. It was a very slack time, they didn't even need the

three of us right then. But anyway, that was that. What could I do? I took the money and packed my bag, and left."

"I hope you didn't walk?"

"No. I got the train. It cost five shillings which was terrible, but I couldn't have walked – it was just too far. It was very cold then. Scotland is colder than here, and there was snow already in some parts. I took the train and arrived in Glasgow in the early evening. I'd written to Seán saying I was coming and luckily he'd got the letter and was at the station to meet me."

"That must have been great."

"It was so wonderful to see him again! There in the big, huge, crowded station, Central Station. I got off the train and it was so strange. All the pistons firing, engines roaring and hissing, wheels clanking. It was such a strange place, I couldn't hear a thing except all those loud noises. And there were people rushing around everywhere. I got off the train and stood on the platform, wondering what on earth I would do next. And the next minute Seán came running along the platform, against the flow of people from the train. We were so happy to be together again! It was the happiest time of my life, that time at the station, with the snow blowing in under the roof and the terrible noise all around us."

Katie stopped talking again and coughed. Sally jumped. She hadn't heard her coughing before, which suddenly struck her as odd. Didn't people who had consumption usually cough a lot of the time? Now Katie had a paroxym of coughs, however. She shook violently and her face turned blue.

"You're tiring yourself out," Mrs Gallagher rushed over to her and put her arms around her. "You should lie down for a while."

"I'm all right," said Katie. "Can I have a drink, please?"

114

Sally poured her a mug of water and handed it to her. Katie drank it gratefully. Then Sally gave her a mug of tea. She calmed down and breathed easily.

"I don't think you should talk any more just now," said her mother. "It's too much of a strain."

"I'd like to tell you everything," said Katie. "I'll take a little rest and then go on."

"I'd better call in Snow and Janey." Sally had forgotten all about them. "It's quite dark now. I hadn't noticed night closing in."

She went out to the yard and called. The moon was already floating across the sky, like a milky white canoe. The northern star twinkled, electric blue, over the ridge of mountains.

"Janey! Snow!"

There was no reply.

"Janey!"

She heard running footsteps and then, from the dark trees at the end of the yard, the two little girls emerged.

"We had such a good time, Sally!" Snow was excited. "We were down at the stream sailing boats under the bridge! Can't we stay there?"

"It's late, Snow," said Sally. " You must come in and go to bed now. Tomorrow you can get up early and play all day long!"

"Do we have to?" asked Janey. "I'm not tired at all."

"You have to."

Sally gave the two girls a mug of milk and some bread, and they went off to bed happily enough. Snow was sharing Janey's little room and bed with her. It was quite a change from her own spacious bedroom in Dublin but she was delighted with it.

Sally and her mother sat down by the fire again.

"You can tell me the rest tomorrow if you like," said Sally. "There's plenty of time."

"I'll go on. There isn't so much more to tell," said Katie. She looked very well again. A rosy flush had come to her cheek. In the soft glow of the firelight she was beautiful.

"You and Seán were at the railway station, in Glasgow?"

"Yes. We left the station after a while and walked around the city, along Saughie Hall Street and Argyll Street and some other. It was very exciting, for me. I'd never been in a big city before, or even a big town, and now I was in one of the biggest cities in Scotland, maybe in the world. The shop windows were all lit with lamps, and full of food and clothes and toys. The streets were packed with people shopping and walking around, rich well-dressed people the like of which I'd never seen, with fur coats and hats, beautiful things. And, of course, a lot of ordinary people and a lot of poor people, too, but I didn't see them at first.

"I was so pleased with everything that Seán didn't tell me the bad news at first. And maybe he was so glad to be with me, as well, that he didn't want to spoil it.

"We got the tram out to where he lived, to Anderson Cross. But as we moved through the streets and got closer to where he lived – the streets changed. They weren't well lit and full of lovely people and shops and horses and carriages any more. They got darker and uglier. There was rubbish all over the ground and a rotten smell everywhere. And when we met people they were not wearing fur coats, but rags. Children with bare feet were running around, begging, even though it was freezing cold. It was snowing, and they were out with no shoes on.

"Anderson. It is the part of Glasgow where most Irish people, most Donegal people, lived. And it is one of the worst parts.

"I was looking around me, feeling dismayed. How could he bear to be in such an ugly place? And then he told me. He had no work. He'd lost his job two weeks before.

"'Why didn't you tell me straight away?' I asked.

"'I hoped I'd get something else,' he said. But there was no work to be had, then. 'It's a bad time,' he said. 'This time of the year. Hundreds of men are laid off from the yards now. But in the New Year there'll be work.'

"Of course I was shocked. I thought I was coming to celebrate Christmas, and get married, and now . . .

"'So how can we get married?' I asked.

"'We can't now,' he said. 'But later it will be all right.'

"'Now I don't even have work,' I said. 'If you'd told me before I could have stayed on the farm. I could have gone on saving money . . . I lost one pound ten by leaving when I did!'

"'I'm sorry,' he said. 'I just couldn't tell you in a letter. I was afraid you'd never marry me if I told you.'

"'How could you think that?' I was very annoyed. Of course I wouldn't have left him just because he was out of work for a while. But it would have been better if he'd got me to send him some money while he was looking for something else. However, 'what's done is done,' I said.

"Then he showed me his lodgings.

"Oh dear God!"

Katie put her hands over her eyes.

"You never saw anything like it. It was a room in a basement, with no furniture except a broken bed and a table. A fire that wasn't lit. It was freezing cold and smelled damp. The walls were all streaked with damp, and mould, and the floorboards were broken in places so there was a draught coming up through them. Later I found out that other things came up too – rats." Katie shuddered.

"Oh dear," said Sally.

"'Couldn't you find something better?' I asked.

"But he said he couldn't. That was the best he could

afford, and most of the rooms for rent in Glasgow, for people like us, were no better.

"So we had to stay there."

"What a Christmas!" said Mrs Gallagher.

"Well, strangely enough, it was. We had a very good time. We had some money, and we believed we would get work in the New Year. The house was cold and damp and infested with rats. The whole street, the whole area, was like that. But the people in the house were very friendly. On Hogmanay a crowd of them came to our door. They came in and drank some whisky with us and then we joined them and went from room to room, in the house, until in the end we were all together. We had a big party. It was great fun. And I was happy to be with Seán."

"That's when you stopped writing to us, isn't it?"

"Yes. I couldn't explain what was going on, could I? And of course I was waiting until I had some good news to send. But I didn't.

"After the New Year Seán went around to all the building sites, to the factories, to the docks and the shipyards, everywhere, looking for work but he couldn't get any. It was a very slack time."

"And you?"

"I got work, in a factory. It was a glove making factory, and I got a job cutting out the gloves."

"So, was that a good job?"

"It paid all right and that was the main thing. But it wasn't very nice – it was a very cold factory, at least at that time of the year. They had no heating at all and our fingers used to get numb, even when working. But I earned a pound a week if I cut the quota of gloves. That was very good money."

"So you managed . . . "

"Oh yes. But Seán wasn't getting anything and he was

getting more and more fed up. He stopped being good humoured and making jokes. I thought we should get married anyway."

"You should have," said Mrs Gallagher.

"But he wouldn't, not until he found something to do. In the end, he got work at the docks, loading and unloading ships, and I changed jobs."

"Why?"

"I got work in another factory, that made tyres for bicycles. That was much better. Then Seán got a job at a warehouse, loading and unloading carts, and we got married."

"You got married? Without telling us?"

"Yes. It all happened quickly, as soon as he got his job. We moved out of the basement into a better room, in the first storey of a big house. It was much cleaner and warmer and had more furniture; then we got married. A few of our friends from the house came to the wedding and were our witnesses."

"When was that?"

"A year and a half ago."

"Oh," said Sally looking closely at Katie. She couldn't believe that so much had gone on in her sister's life – so much that she knew nothing about.

"Well, everything seemed fine for a while. Seán was doing well at the warehouse and I was much happier at the rubber factory than I had been in the terrible glovemaking place. But then . . . "

Katie stopped dead for a second.

"Seán died."

"Oh Katie!"

"Aye. He was killed at work. A load of bricks that was being taken off a ship with a crane fell on his head. That was that."

"Oh Katie. And you still never told us?"

"No. I'd got out of the habit of writing by then and so much . . . so much had happened. I was so far away. I'm sorry, but I'd nearly forgotten about you all. You just all seemed so far away."

"We were here. We still are."

"Yes, I know. Well, I had my job, at least, and I had a few friends from the old house although I hadn't made friends in the new place yet. The trouble was I couldn't afford to stay there. The rent was too high for me on my own. So I moved again, to a very small room, in a basement. Basements were the cheapest, but this one was not too bad."

"And you went on working?"

"There was no trouble about that. The rubber factory was doing very well and I was good at the work. But the next thing was, I found out I was expecting a baby. And after a while I couldn't hide it any more and I had to give up the work, and then I had no money at all apart from the bit I'd saved."

"Oh dear, dear."

"I thought I'd have to come home then. I thought I'd use the money I had to get a train ticket and boat fare and come home."

"Why didn't you?"

"I got very sick. I got so sick I couldn't do anything. A woman who was our friend came to visit me and brought me to the hospital, and I was in hospital for five months."

"Oh, Katie. I can't believe you didn't write!"

"I lost the baby. And in the end they let me out and then I did come home."

"And they told you you have consumption?"

"No," said Katie. "They told me they thought I had a shadow on the lung."

120

"What is a shadow on the lung but consumption?" said Mrs Gallagher, sadly.

"Maybe they're wrong," said Sally.

"Katie, you have to go to bed now," said Mrs Gallagher. "It's the middle of the night. Sally must be worn out too."

"I am," said Sally. "Goodnight, mother. Goodnight, Katie. We can talk more tomorrow. Goodnight, my dear, my dear!"

Sixteen

The Post Mistress

Katie stayed in bed late the next morning.

"She sleeps until ten or eleven o'clock," explained Mrs Gallagher to Sally. She and Packy, Sally, Snow and Janey were having a breakfast of porridge at the kitchen table. "She needs as much rest as she can get, poor pet."

"She has had a very hard time," said Sally. "And she looks very weak. But maybe she doesn't have consumption?"

"That's what I've been telling your mammy ever since the wee lass came home but she won't listen to me," said Packy.

"Well, I don't know. God knows it's what I want to believe. But I've seen many a girl with that ailment in my day and I think I know it when I see it."

"Has she been to the doctor?"

"No, no, not yet," said Mrs Gallagher, sounding confused. "She's only home a few weeks and she said she didn't want the doctor yet."

"All the same," said Sally, trying to mask her impatience, "it might be a good idea to get the doctor and ask him what he thinks."

"Divil a need for a doctor," said Packy. "Some fresh air and good food and she'll be as right as rain. That's what I'm after telling your mammy all along. Sure anybody would get sick in Glasgow."

"Were you ever there?" asked Sally politely.

"Indeed and I was not, Sally, and thanks be to the good Lord for that. But me brother was there and me sister Nellie and do you know the things they told me about yon place would make the hairs on your head stand on end so they would, they would aye," Packy slurped down his porridge.

"Can we go out now, Sally?" asked Snow, who had been listening to all of this with great interest. "You said we could go up the mountain?"

"Yes," said Sally. "And we will. But first I am sending a message to the doctor. I think we have to have Katie looked at. It's ridiculous to keep her here not knowing what is wrong with her or how to treat her."

"The doctor costs a lot of money, Sally," said her mother warningly.

"I know," Sally said brightly. "But don't worry. I'll pay for it if need be."

"I don't want to be taking your money off you, Sally. I'm sure it's hard earned. Sure, I haven't even had time to ask you how you're getting on in Dublin at all."

"Do you think my money is hard earned, Snow?" Sally winked at her pupil.

"I don't know," said Snow, which was a very tactful answer, for her. "I'll go out and play by the river while I'm waiting for you. All right?"

"That's all right, Snow," Sally said. "Don't fall in if you can help it. I'll call you when I'm ready."

Sally scribbled a note.

"I'll walk up to the post office with this," she said, "and leave it there for Hughie Tinney. He'll take it to the doctor when he's on his way to Rathmullan with the post."

"Whatever you say, Sally," said her mother, rather

meekly. It was clear that Sally was going to have her way on this issue, and in a way it was a great relief to Mrs Gallagher to have someone share the burden with. Packy had not been much use, telling her there was nothing wrong with Katie and that everything would be all right. It was much better having somebody who would take some practical measures to deal with the problem.

"I'll bring Katie up her breakfast now," she added.

"Does she have a good appetite?" Sally asked.

"Not very good, but she eats, all right," said her mother.

"That's a good sign," said Sally, who knew that consumptive patients often had no appetite at all.

She left the house and walked to the stream. It was a small babbling brook, which flowed from a spring in the mountain down to the valley, and then made a beeline for the beach. Just behind Sally's house the stream passed under a stone bridge, as it crossed the road, and Snow was at this bridge, playing with Janey. They were under it, in fact, throwing twigs into the water and watching them bob along downstream on the chestnut-coloured water.

Sally went down to the edge of the water. She had often played in this stream herself when she was a little girl, doing exactly what Snow was doing. It had been a great game and she had always loved it. Now when she called gently to Snow the latter jumped. She had been concentrating so fiercely on her game.

"Hello, Sally," she said. "It's lovely here, isn't it? Much better than the park."

"I'm glad you like it," said Sally. The golden brown brook, the loops of vivid green watercress sprouting from its waters, the graceful rushes, the yellow flag lilies on the bank: who would not like it all? She listened to the music of the stream, that most light-hearted of all music, and breathed deeply the crystal clean air. "I like it too. But now we're going on a walk to the post office."

"I'd rather stay here," said Snow.

"I know" said Sally. "But you can't. You must come with me and Janey has to go home to help Mammy. And later we'll do something more exciting."

To her astonishment, Snow came leaping up from under the bridge. The country air had changed her character and made her obedient. Or maybe it was that she knew that here she was dependent on Sally for everything, and had better stay in her good books?

The pair walked along the road through Glenbra to the village, where the post office was.

It was a lovely summer's day. The hedges were foaming with hawthorn, white and pink, and the ditches bejewelled with primroses and violets. In some fields the new crop of oats was sprouting, a fresh pale airy green, and in others the sky blue tinge of flax already showed. Sheep and lambs baaed from the hillside.

Sally met one or two neighbours, and stopped to exchange a few words with them. Everyone was surprised to see her home, and they wanted to know how Katie was and what was wrong with her. Sally tried to tell them the truth, that Katie was not well but that they were not sure what was the matter with her. The neighbours looked suspicious. Sally knew what they were thinking: that Katie had T.B. but that she wouldn't admit it. She could not blame them for suspecting that. The fact was that people often tried to disguise the truth where this illness was concerned. They were ashamed to have it in their families, as if it reflected badly on them. People believed you contracted it because you didn't have enough to eat, or because you lived in bad, damp conditions. And everyone was ashamed to have to acknowledge that this might be true, even at a time when a great many people did live in terrible conditions.

When she reached the post office there were further

enquiries from old Hannah, the postmistress. She was a little dumpling of a woman, with grey curly hair and glasses perched on the edge of her nose. Her inquisitiveness was well-known.

"Oh, is that you, Sally Gallagher?" she said. Her voice was high and girlish, for a woman aged about seventy. "It seems like no time at all since you left for Dublin. And who is this lady?"

Sally introduced Snow, who was gazing happily at the musty little post office.

"Ah, I see. You are here on a wee holiday then, is that it?"

"I came home because Katie is not well," said Sally, making a clean breast of it. With people like Hannah, it was always best to tell them what they wanted to hear straight away. You would have to tell them eventually, anyway.

"So I hear, so I hear. Poor wee Katie. She was always a lovely girl."

"We're getting the doctor for her," said Sally. "I'm leaving this note here so that Hughie can take it in to him when he goes with the post."

"Is that so? Is that so? She must be bad, then," said Hannah.

"She's quite well, I think," said Sally. "I'd like the doctor to have a look at her, that's all."

"Oh that's all. A look at her. That's all," repeated Hannah, taking the note and scrutinising it as if she might be able to get some more information just from an examaination of its shape. It was obvious from her tone that she did not believe for one moment that Katie was not dangerously ill. Why else would anyone get the doctor?

She put the letter on a shelf behind the counter, where she had her brass weighing scales and various stamps and pens. Then she turned to Sally again.

"And how are you getting on in Dublin?"

"The best," said Sally. "I like it very much."

"It'll be a change for you," said Hannah. "After all that happened here."

"What's that?" said Sally, with a widening of her eyes.

"Oh, now I know you didn't have it all that easy, Sally my dear. But it is great that you are making a go of it all the same. I suppose you make a lot of money down there?"

"A bit," said Sally, preparing to leave.

"I saw your young man only today," Hannah said, noticing that Sally was about to escape and trying to hold her back.

"My young man?" Sally stopped, with her hand on the doorknob. She could hardly believe her ears.

"That Manus fellow. He and you were very great, weren't you, until he started going with that other one, the doctor's daughter?"

"Goodbye, Hannah," said Sally firmly, although she felt as if a big hand had clamped over her throat and was throttling her. "Come on Snow, we have to go."

"Goodbye Sally," said Hannah. "I didn't . . . I hope . . . "
Sally banged the door.

In the lane outside the post office she sat on a wall for a few minutes to catch her breath.

"Why are you sitting there, Sally? Don't you feel well?"

"I'll be all right in a minute," said Sally. "Just be patient."

"What's wrong?"

"I'm not sure," said Sally. She wasn't. It surprised her that a few words could have such a profound effect on her. How could the very name Manus, uttered by somebody like Hannah, make her whole body change? Her heart was pounding, her blood was racing, she felt as if she might collapse.

Sit still. Sit still. It's just words, she told herself.

She sat there for five minutes.

Then she felt all right again, and she and Snow set out for home.

Seventeen

The Water Horse

"I asked the doctor to call tomorrow morning, if possible," said Sally.

Katie was sitting in the big chair, by the open window. She was wrapped in the big black shawl to keep out the cold. But a fresh light breeze blew through the window, with the tang of cowslips and the sea on it. She could see the hens with their yellow chicks pecking among the stones of the yard, and beyond them the spreading sycamores, their leaves light and joyous as brand new summer frocks and beyond them, in the distance, the sapphire gleam of the sea.

"This is all the doctor I need," Katie waved at the view.

"You may be right, but I want him to come all the same," said Sally.

"It's very very good of you," Katie spoke seriously. "And very brave."

She remembered, as did everyone, that Manus had been walking out with the doctor's daughter, Eileen, ever since he had abandoned Sally.

Sally felt a familiar sinking of her heart.

"I always liked Dr Carr," she said. "He's a good, kind

man. I'll never forget how well he looked after Bridgie's little boy when he was so sick. And never got a penny for it."

Bridgie was a poor widow who had been evicted from her home a few years before. Sally had become friendly with her and helped her as much as she could, especially when her little boy was sick. Dr Carr had been very helpful then too, but had been unable to save the boy, who died.

"Poor Bridgie. I wonder how she is? I must drop in to see her."

Snow came into the kitchen.

"All right, Snow," said Sally. "You've been very patient. We're going now."

"Can Janey come with us?"

"She's away over the road somewhere," said Sally. "Maybe she can follow us later, when she gets back. But I think we should start now."

Sally packed some bread and butter, and a bottle of cold sweet tea, in a basket. She and Snow put on their jackets and boots, and tied cotton squares on their heads.

"Tell Janey we're taking the turf road, up to the harebell brae," said Sally to Katie.

"I wish . . . "

"You wish you could come too?" Sally gave her sister a kiss. "Of course you do. But if you sit here, and breathe the good air, and drink plenty of milk, who knows? Soon you will be able to do everything, just as if nothing had happened to you."

"I'll never be able to do that," said Katie. "Such a lot has happened."

"That's true. But you might get well again. Life is full of fresh starts," Sally smiled philosophically. "And now, goodbye until teatime!"

Sally and Snow went to the stream. There, just beside the bridge, was a barbed wire gate tied with a piece of rope.

Sally undid the rope and let Snow through, and then tied it up again. They found themselves on a narrow road. The middle part of the road was covered with grass, and the sides were clay and stones. The road was used by Packy and a few other farmers when they went up the hill to cut turf. Today, however, it was, as often, deserted.

They began to walk. At first the road was not steep and it was easy to cover ground. Snow bounded along. The air was full of delicate, mountain sounds: dripping water and babbling brooks, curlews calling and lapwings saying "peewee, peewee, peewee." They saw a falcon, hovering high above the boggy mountain for minutes on end, and then diving like a stone to the ground.

"Poor little thing," said Sally.

"The falcon?"

"No, the mouse or the little bird or whatever he dived on."

"Ah!" said Snow, turning her gaze to the sky with renewed interest.

After the first stretch the gradient grew steeper and walking became climbing. Snow kept it up for about ten minutes before declaring, "I'm tired! How far is it to that place you said we were going to?"

"Harebell Brae? It's about another mile," Sally smiled. "We've barely started."

"Oh," said Snow. "Better keep going, then."

"Do you know any songs?" asked Sally.

"Ta ra ra boom de ray

My knickers flew away

They will come back some day

Ta ra ra boom de ay!"

sang Snow, in clear innocent tones.

"Mm," said Sally. "Very nice. Let me think of something."

130

She walked along, wondering what she could sing that would make climbing easier.

"Aililiu na gamhna, na gamhna bana,"

she sang.

"Alliliu na gamhna, na gamhna siad ab fhearr liom!"

"What does it mean?" asked Snow.

"It means *Allililu* the cows, the white cows, *alliliu* the cows, the cows I love the best!"

"Silly song!" said Snow.

"Well, what about Ta ra ra boom de ray! That's pretty silly too."

"At least it's funny," said Snow. "The one about the cows is just silly and not funny. There is a difference. Can we have a rest?"

"We're only about one third of the way," Sally said. She stood and looked down. Below her spread the valley of Glenbra, with its network of fields and tiny houses, its warrens of roads and paths, stretching from the hills to the diamond shaped lough. On the other shore of the lough were more mountains and long yellow beaches. A few of the larger buildings were visible, in particular a long, white house with a white tower at one end. Sally had always wondered what it was and who lived there. It was strange, seeing a house so clearly almost every day of your life while you were growing up, and not knowing anything at all about who lived in it.

"All right," said Sally. She sat down and pulled out some of the bread. She was feeling quite tired herself.

"Maybe we won't climb as far as Heather Brae after all . . . "

"Harebell Brae."

"Sorry, Harebell Brae. Maybe we'll just go to the next brae."

"It looks like the top of the mountain, just there."

"It looks like it. But it isn't. When you get to the top of

131

that ridge you see there is another slope ahead of you. And when you get to that one there is another slope ahead of that. And so on. There are many, many slopes like this, before you get to the top of this mountain. And it is a low mountain."

"What do you see if you get to the top?"

"First, you see lakes, and they are very beautiful. They are black and deep, right in the middle of the mountain. Some people say they are bottomless. If you fall in you will never be found, but will go right down into the centre of the earth and come out somewhere in the southern part of the globe."

"Goodness me! Do you believe that?"

"Well . . . Other people say there is a monster in the lake. Not a monster – a horse. A fairy horse."

"I've never heard of a fairy horse," said Snow, munching her bread.

Sally tried to recall the legend she had heard about the lake.

"They say that a farmer down in the valley, just down there in that house, do you see?"

She pointed to a cottage not far from where they sat.

"He had a few fields and two cows. One summer he noticed that there was not much grass on his fields and he began to be suspicious of his neighbours. He thought they were grazing their cattle on his grass at night, when he was asleep."

"Funny thing to do!"

"Yes. But people around here can be very suspicious. Anyway, he decided to see if this was happening. So he waited up one night, hiding in the ditch. He waited and waited, for hours and was about to go back to bed when he heard horse's hooves. And he saw two beautiful horses, a pitch black foal and its mother, a mare as white as snow, coming cantering down this path here that we are walking on now. And the horses came down into his field and started eating the grass.

He sneaked back to his barn and got two halters. And he came back and tried to catch the horses. As soon as they heard him they started to race off. But he managed to catch the foal. The mare escaped and ran back up the hill.

The foal grew up and became the most wonderful horse anyone around here had ever seen. It could pull a cart and a plough, and it could race along the white sands, and no horse could beat it. It was a beautiful, shining, black horse, with a white star on its forehead.

People came from all around to see it. And many people offered to buy it. But the farmer refused to sell. He didn't need to, because he won a lot of money on the horse, in races.

One day he was drawing turf from up here, from up near Harebell Brae, I think, or maybe even a bit higher, and he brought this horse with him, instead of the old ass. The horse started to get restless as they came up the mountain. He had to keep a tight rein on him. Then, when they got up near the top, he began to hear a loud whinnying. Another horse was whinnying and whinnying, from up in the middle of the mountain. And the black horse became more and more frisky and difficult to hold back. In the end the black horse broke away from him, and raced into the middle of the mountain. He followed as fast as he could, and the last thing he saw of the black horse, was it leaping into the lake, to join its mother, the white horse, there in the middle of the lake, waiting for him. Then the two of them sank into the lake and they've never been seen again since in these parts."

"Maybe they are in Australia," said Snow, dreamily.

"Maybe they are," agreed Sally.

"I'd love to see those lakes," said Snow.

"Well, it won't be easy, if we climb so slowly," said Sally. "Look, there's Janey already, coming up to join us!"

"Will we go down and join her instead?" asked Snow. "We've walked so much already."

"Very well," said Sally, looking wistfully at the next slope. "If you are tired."

"I am tired, Sally," said Snow, seriously. "And there is something else that I must tell you, something very important that I think you have forgotten."

Sally was alarmed.

"What can that be?"

"Tomorrow."

"Tomorrow?"

"Tomorrow is my birthday."

Eighteen

A Surprise Visit

Sally had forgotten all about Snow's eleventh birthday. In the country, people never celebrated birthdays at all. She understood that Snow would not appreciate that very much.

She managed to retrieve the situation by asking her mother to bake some gooseberry pies, which they had for tea. Snow was pleased, especially as the postman had brought her a letter and a big parcel containing a beautiful doll, as well as some other gifts, from Dublin.

"Mamma did not forget!" she cried happily. "She did not forget!"

The doll was a collector's item – one of the ones Snow had selected months earlier, when she had been in Grafton Street with Mrs Erikson. It was a lovely doll, but Snow was more delighted by the fact of her mother having remembered both her birthday and her interest in this particular doll than the present itself. She was in the best of spirits.

"There is a letter for you, too," Snow said, handing Sally an envelope.

The letter, in Mrs Erikson's bold heavy hand, urged Sally

to stay on for as long as necessary in Donegal. But she wanted Snow to come home in not later than two weeks' time.

"Your mother would like you to come home," Sally said cautiously.

"I don't want to go!" wailed Snow.

"Well, you won't have to go for a while anyway," Sally said. "And, depending on what the doctor says tomorrow, I may be able to travel with you."

Mrs Gallagher looked upset but said nothing.

Sally went out for a walk to think things over. She realised that if she stayed at home for very much longer she might be in danger of losing her job in Dublin. The Eriksons were very kind, but in September they would need somebody to look after Snow again. Sally could not expect them to wait forever for her to return.

Part of her already missed Dublin – she had carved out such a full life for herself there, already. When she thought of Ethel and Thomas, her penny-farthing bicycle, the play she was missing out on because of her sudden visit to Donegal, she longed to pack her bags and return on the next train. On the other hand, she loved being at home with her mother and sisters, and she wanted to help Katie as much as she could.

She decided to wait until the doctor saw Katie before she made up her mind about her own plans.

When she returned to the house there was a surprise visitor for Sally.

Manus.

"Sally," said Mrs Gallagher, when Sally came in, red in the face and invigorated by her walk. "Manus has called around to see you."

Mrs Gallagher was very confused, but not half as confused as Sally.

"Hello Sally," he said, in a shy voice. "How are you?"

"Very well, thank you," Sally said. She sounded much more composed than she felt.

"I'll run out and . . . collect the eggs," said Mrs Gallagher, trying to think of a reason to leave them alone together. But they wouldn't be alone anyway. Sally looked despairingly at the curtained bed, where Granny lay. Maybe asleep and maybe awake.

"Is that Sally?" the old voice came from behind the curtains, putting paid to her hope.

"Yes, Granny!" said Sally.

She went over to the old woman and clasped her hand for a minute.

"Granny! I'll be back to you very soon. I'm busy for a little while."

"I never see you," said the old woman. "And when I do you are always rushing away somewhere. Young people are always so busy. I was never busy. Never was and never will be."

Sally returned to Manus.

"Would you like to take a walk?" he said, tactfully.

"Oh yes," said Sally. "I'd love to take a walk, I need one."

In her confusion she forgot that she had just come back from a long walk up the mountain.

They left the house and walked down towards the sea.

"Sally," said Manus. "It's such a long time since I saw you. I've missed you."

"Have you?" asked Sally. She looked at him. He was still so handsome that he took her breath away. Or maybe he was not so handsome. But for some reason there would never be anyone who would have the same effect on her as Manus. There was something about him which made her feel that he was the man in the world who had been made for her. She felt that they were two sides of one thing, one apple.

"Oh yes, very much," he said. "I tried to write to you. I got your address from Hannah at the post office. And I wrote two or three letters."

"I never got them," said Sally.

"I never posted them," said Manus. "I Couldn't. I tore them up."

"Oh!" Sally felt impatient. It was no good. Letters that were not posted were no good, to her or to anybody. It was no good even telling her about them, even though she could understand why he might have done it.

"I'm sorry," Manus said again. "I would understand if you never wanted to see me again."

"I'll always want to see you again," said Sally, with in inner sigh. It would be better for her if she never wanted to see him again.

"What is it like, in Dublin?"

"Nice. Different," she said. "It is so different that I could hardly begin to explain."

"I've never been there," said Manus.

"You have never been to Dublin?" Sally stared at him. She was so used to thinking of Manus as somebody immeasurably superior to her that the idea of his experience being more limited, in any way, than hers, shocked her.

"Well, no," said Manus. "Most people around here haven't been."

"Has Eileen Carr?"

Manus blushed.

"Yes, she has."

"Are you still . . . ?"

"Not really," he said.

Sally's heart sank. She had hoped he would say "No."

"What does that mean, 'not really'?"

"It means I see her occasionally, but it's over . . . there is nothing between us, if there ever was."

This made Sally feel better.

"And is that how she feels too?"

"I think so. She's been walking out with somebody else, I believe."

"Ah," said Sally.

They walked along the little green lane in silence for a minute. The turbulent emotions they had both felt when they met first had calmed down a bit. Sally felt her head getting lighter and clearer.

She decided to wait for him to speak next.

But when he did it was just to ask

"What do you do, exactly, in Dublin?"

"I teach that child, Snow, whom you saw at my house. I'm a governess at her house."

"Some big house in Dublin?"

"Yes, it is a very big house by Glenbra standards. They have another servant, and a lot of lovely things."

"Do you spend all your time there? Do you see other people?"

Sally knew what he was trying to find out.

"I have friends. I see a lot of people, yes. I belong to a group that is doing a play and I have a part in that play – at least, I hope I still do. And I go out cycling with some friends, Ethel and Thomas, they are called."

"You can ride a bicycle?"

"I've just learned! I can even ride a penny-farthing. Thomas and Ethel have been calling me 'Penny-farthing Sally', because I am the only person in Dublin who rides one nowadays."

"I can't imagine you on a bicycle. I saw a motor car the other day for the first time. They are unbelievable, aren't they?"

"Yes. Amazing."

"I suppose there are hundreds of them in Dublin?"

"Oh no . . . Not at all. I've only seen one or two, actually. Most people go around on bicycles, or in jaunting cars, or cabs."

"I'd love to go there," Manus said.

"Well, it is nice," Sally said lamely. "But of course here is nice too. Everywhere has its advantages."

They had reached the shore. At their feet the river, which separated the road from the beach, bubbled along. The stepping stones to the beach invited them.

"Will we walk on the shore for a minute?" asked Manus.

"Yes," said Sally.

She picked her way across the stones. When she was half way across she put her foot on a wobbly stone. Manus reached out to steady her. He put his hand on her back and clasped her waist.

Then he drew her to him and kissed her.

"Sally," he said. They were standing on a wobbling stone in the middle of the river. "I love you. Will you marry me?"

The stone wobbled back and forth.

"I'll . . . I'll have to think about it," said Sally.

She kissed him again.

Nineteen

The Doctor Calls

Sally hardly slept a wink all night.

She lay in bed, with several versions of her future life playing themselves out in her head.

She saw herself as Manus's wife, in a farmhouse in Glenbra. She was dressed in a black skirt and a white blouse, with a big apron over it all. Her sleeves were rolled up and she was digging into a big sack of meal, getting fodder for the fowl. She was going to the byre to milk the cows. She saw herself crouched on a three legged stool, her head pressed to the hot, bony flank of a red and white cow.

She saw herself dressed in a white lace dress, walking out of Glenbra Chapel on Manus's arm. There were flowers in her hair and in his button hole. They were surrounded by flowers, and happy laughter.

She saw herself in Dublin, sitting at a drawing room window – a window very like the Eriksons'. It was a big bay window, with a vase of fragrant freesias in it, and a view of a shady garden. The garden was surrounded by laurel bushes, closing over, almost hiding, a silver gate. At the gate was Thomas. Thomas was opening the gate, walking up a wide gravelled driveway to the flight of steps that led to the door.

Sally had on a pale silk dress – one of those elaborate dresses made of exotic materials called *mousseline* or *crepe de chine* that she saw in the shop windows. Her hair was piled on her head in bunches of curls. Her long fingers shone under rings – sapphires, diamonds and rubies.

She saw herself and Thomas in the foyer of a theatre. She saw herself and him on a bicycle, one bicycle, like the tandems one sometimes saw in Dublin. A bicycle made for two.

She saw herself as a maid in a kitchen, like Biddy, a fat old maid, with a cross face, scrubbing the floor and hanging out the washing.

When she finally slept she dreamt her castle dream.

She is in a big grey fairytale castle, with turrets and towers and a drawbridge. The castle is full of rooms, one more splendid than the next. Rooms carpeted with red carpets from Turkey and Persia, rooms hung with glittering chandeliers, rooms filled with gleaming polished furniture and gold and silver goblets. The castle is shining, resplendent, and somewhere in the castle a great feast is going on. Sally is at the feast and Manus should be there too. The guests, in their dresses of silk and velvet, their red satin suits, their gleaming tiaras, flock around tables laden with delicious food and wine. Sally is there among them but she is not able to eat or drink, she is not able to dance or talk. She is looking for Manus. She knows he was here just a moment ago, that she has just missed him. She runs from room to room, certain that he is in the castle and all that she has to do is look a little longer.

And then he is there.

He is there, sitting on a wooden chair in a little room in the basement of the castle.

He holds out his arms and she falls into them.

This is not how the dream ends, as a rule.

Sally woke up, smiling.

Her mother was knocking on her door.

"Sally," she said urgently. "It's so late! Dr Carr is here"

Sally sprang out of bed and threw on her clothes. She pulled a brush through her tangled hair and tied it back with a ribbon. Then she straightened up Katie's bed and dashed out.

"Good morning, Dr Carr," she said. "Sorry to keep you. I didn't expect you so early."

"Good morning, Sally. It's nice to see you again." The tall, grey bearded doctor smiled kindly at Sally. Not for the first time she wished he did not have to be the father of her rival, Eileen.

"Thank you very much for coming," Sally shook his hand.

"Of course I had to come. May I see the patient now?"

"Yes, come this way," Sally led the doctor and her mother into Katie's room.

"You know Katie?" Sally asked. "She has had a difficult time, working in a factory and living in a damp, terrible place in Glasgow. And she is coughing . . . "

"Maybe Katie can tell me about it?" the doctor suggested.

Sally and her mother left the room.

They waited in the kitchen, biting their fingernails, for almost half an hour.

"What can be keeping him so long?" Mrs Gallagher wondered.

"He's probably asking her a lot of questions," replied Sally, trying to be as sensible as possible. But she too felt very anxious.

At last the doctor emerged.

He walked into the kitchen in silence and put his black bag heavily on the table.

"Sit down for a minute," he said to Sally and her mother, who had stood up when he came in.

They sat down. He pulled a chair up from the table and sat beside them.

"Well," he said. "I'll tell you exactly what I have found. Katie is very weak, very weak indeed. She has had a very bad dose of pleurisy while in Glasgow, and it hasn't been very well treated. The result is that she has a slight puncture in the lung."

"Consumption?" said Sally.

"Yes, I'm afraid so," said the doctor.

"I knew it," said Mrs Gallagher. "Those high red spots . . . "

"It is in the very, very early stages," said the doctor. "And there is hope for her. It may not be fatal."

"No?"

"If she gets proper care and rest, she might live for a long time . . . maybe not into old age, but a long time."

"Oh doctor," said Mrs Gallagher. "What good is that to a young girl with all before her?"

"Poor Katie," said the doctor. "She has a lot behind her, too."

"She told you everything?" said Sally.

"Yes," said the doctor. "Or a lot of it, anyway. She's lucky that she had the sense to come home. If she'd stayed in Glasgow she wouldn't be alive now."

"So what should we do?"

"Just do what you are doing already. Feed her well and make sure she gets a lot of fresh air. And no getting cold or damp." He stood up. "The sea air will be good for her. You never know, by winter she might be almost recovered."

"Should she go to hospital?"

"No," said the doctor. "She is much better off here than in any hospital you could find. If she could go to a

144

sanatorium in Switzerland, maybe, that would be good. But as she can't, this is better than a hospital."

Mrs Gallagher was crying now. Sally was grief stricken, but she did not cry.

"I have to go now," he said. "I have other calls to make."

"How much do I owe you?" Sally asked.

"It's all right for this time," he said. "I'll call again next week. Don't worry about the money."

"Thank you so much, Doctor," said Sally, clasping his hand in deep gratitude.

Katie got up and came into the kitchen.

She was much more cheerful than either Sally or her mother.

"He said he thought I might get well," she said, stretching joyfully by the window.

"Yes, he did," Sally turned to her, questioningly.

"I know I am going to get better!" said Katie. "I feel it in my bones!"

"I'll take care of you," Mrs Gallagher came over and hugged her.

"And so will I," said Sally.

But she did not quite know how she was going to do this.

Twenty

Back in Dublin

Doctor Carr's words decided Sally. She would go back to the Eriksons with Snow, and stay with them for a while, at least. She knew that her mother and Katie could manage without her for the time being. Besides, she wanted to spend some time away from Manus, for reasons which she found difficult to put her finger on.

They returned to Dublin two weeks later. Snow was as brown as a berry, and her name was more inappropriate than ever.

"How wonderful you look!" exclaimed her mother. "Like a little picaninni!"

Mrs Erikson, Professor Erikson and Sam had spent most of the summer in Dublin.

"I felt so poorly, I couldn't bear to leave my doctor," said Mrs Erikson. "And good old Sam and Erik stayed with me to keep me company."

"Of course we did, Mamma," said Sam. But he told Snow that he had had a very dull summer and he was really glad to be getting back to school in England.

Mrs Erikson cried copiously before he left, much to his dismay.

"I'll be back soon," the tall, thin boy, in his black suit, comforted her. "Soon it will be Christmas, and I'll be home."

"I know, I know," sobbed Mrs Erikson. "I don't know why I feel so sad. I suppose it is because we have had such a long lovely summer together."

"Yes, Mamma, and I am sad too. But be brave! Soon I will be back."

A few days after Sally returned she had a letter from Thomas, asking if she could see him.

Sally wrote a reply and put it in her pocket, with the intention of posting it the next day. She did so, but before Thomas could have received it he was around at the house anyway, accompanied by Ethel.

"Sally! You went off without telling us a thing!" exclaimed Ethel. "What a low thing to do!"

"I'm sorry," said Sally. "I was called home very suddenly."

"Is anything wrong?" asked Thomas gently. He was wearing a new, dark, sober suit in some sort of soft material, and a soft black cap. He looked gentler and more sombre than ever.

"Yes," Sally replied simply. "My sister Katie, the one who was in Glasgow, has come home. She is very ill."

"Oh dear," Ethel made a moue of sympathy. "Nothing too serious, I hope."

"Well, she might recover, and she might not. She was looking well, when I left."

Suddenly Sally felt like crying. In the heel of the hunt, it had been very hard to say goodbye to her mother and sister. And to Manus. She was still not sure if she had done the right thing or not.

"Poor Sally! Well, there's bad news here as well."

"What's that?"

"You've lost your part in the play!"

147

Sally laughed.

"Oh dear! I thought it was something really serious! I think I can cope with the loss of the part."

"I'm doing it instead!" said Ethel. "I hope you don't mind. I tried to get them to keep it but they said no. The play is going on in a few weeks' time."

"The rehearsal period seems to be very long!" said Thomas.

"Well, since we only rehearse once or twice a week, it takes a long time."

"That's great, Ethel," said Sally. "I hope I can go to the play when it is on."

"Good!" Ethel grinned. "Actually, we wondered if you would like to come for a spin, on the bike?"

It was seven o'clock in the evening, still quite bright. Sally felt a bit too sad and confused to go out cycling.

"So, will you come with us? You must use Mother's bike, of course!"

"All right" said Sally. "I'll just get my hat!"

She went out with Ethel and Thomas and the trio cycled, three abreast, all down the long, winding Palmerston Road, down Charleston Road into Ranelagh and back up by Milltown to the back of the park.

At the railings Ethel stopped.

"Like to pop inside?" she teased.

"No thank you," said Sally. "Once was enough for me."

"In that case, time for bed," said Ethel.

"All right. I'll bring this bicycle back," said Sally.

"No need to do that, Sally," said Thomas, winking furiously at Ethel. "I'll go home with you and then I can wheel the bike back to Ethel, you know the way I do."

He meant, cycling on one bike while pulling the other alongside with one hand.

"Goodnight then!" sang Ethel, already halfway down the street. "Sleep sweetly!"

Thomas and Sally cycled slowly back to the Erikson's house.

At the gate Sally dismounted.

"Here you are!" she said gaily. And hopefully. She did not want to have a serious talk with Thomas just at this moment. "Goodnight!"

"Sally!" said Thomas. "I need to talk to you."

"Well, that's fine," Sally continued to be cheery. "Talk away!"

"I mean . . . could you meet me tomorrow night? Could you come out with me, alone with me, somewhere?"

"Where?" asked Sally.

"I don't know. I'll think of something. Could you have tea with me in a restaurant, something like that? Or just go for a walk?"

"I think so," said Sally. "If the Eriksons will let me off, I will."

"That's fair enough," Thomas smiled in relief. "I'll call for you at about seven o'clock tomorrow, then. If the Eriksons let you off. And if they don't . . . "

He made a cut throat sign with his hand, and walked away pushing the bikes.

149

Twenty-One

The Boer War

But before Thomas could fulfil his yearning, cherished all summer long, of having Sally to himself for a whole evening, a new event distrupted life in the Erikson household.

There had been changes since Sally and Snow had returned. Snow was attending classes at a school for young ladies this year. This meant that Sally did not have any teaching duties in the mornings. Instead, she helped Biddy with the housework, or acted as a personal companion to Mrs Erikson. That was how Mrs Erikson described it. What it meant was that Sally went shopping with her, and to the dressmakers. She spent long hours discussing with Mrs Erikson the merits of one hat as opposed to another, or whether blue suited her better than purple. She also carried a lot of parcels. Mrs Erikson was a passionate shopper.

The day after Thomas' invitation to Sally, she and Mrs Erikson spent the morning in Sackville Street, visiting the shops there – Mrs Erikson was searching for new material for curtains for the drawing-room.

"The old ones have been there for eighteen years," she said. "I am so weary of them."

The old curtains were heavy green velvet with long golden fringes. Sally thought they were very attractive.

"I want something much lighter and brighter!" gushed Mrs Erikson. "I want something which reminds me of the sky and the sun, of the spring and the light. I can't bear the thought of struggling through the winter shut in by those dismal colours."

"No," said Sally quietly.

The morning had been spent in the big haberdashery departments. Roll after heavy roll of cloth – velvet and brocade, cotton and satin – had been pulled from shelves by stoical, stern-faced men in black suits. Every roll had been fondled and pulled, held up to the light and up to the dark. Some had been carried to the doorway and examined in daylight. And in the end Mrs Erikson had said:

"Perhaps the green velvet is not so bad, after all, Sally. What do you think?"

"Oh," Sally was at a loss. Sometimes it was not easy to know what Mrs Erikson expected her to think. "Perhaps not. The fringes give it a light effect."

"That is so true, Sally. The fringes do indeed give it a light effect. Yes," she turned to the shop assistant, who had been attending her for almost two hours. "I have decided not to make a purchase today, after all. I must reconsider my colour scheme."

"Very well, Madam." The shop assistant, a middle aged man with a long black moustache and slicked down hair, placed a roll of cloth on the cutting table with a heavy thud. "Good day to you." He turned on his heel and walked away.

"What a rude man!" Mrs Erikson pouted. "I should complain to the manager."

But she did not. Instead, she and Sally took the tram and went home.

When they arrived in Palmerston Park, Biddy met them at the hall door. She looked nervous and alarmed.

"Oh Missus," she exclaimed "A telegram arrived just after you left this morning. I couldn't think what to do!"

"Give it to me now, Biddy, give it to me now!" Mrs Erikson demanded impatiently.

Biddy ran down the hall to the kitchen and came up, panting, clutching the telegram.

Mrs Erikson opened it and scanned it.

Then she fell on the floor in a faint.

"Glory be to God, Sally, the missus is dead!" Biddy bent over Mrs Erikson. Her eyes rolled and she lay, white as a sheet, flat out on the floor.

"Get some water, Biddy," Sally ordered. She knelt down beside Mrs Erikson and slapped her face. Nothing happened. She shook her shoulders. Nothing happened. Then Biddy returned, very red, with a jug of water. Sally poured some into Mrs Erikson's mouth and a little on her temples.

Her eyes opened slowly.

"I will get up . . . I am having such a strange dream . . . "

Her voice was slurred.

"Where am I? Mother?"

"Wake up, Mrs Erikson, wake up. You fainted."

"My smelling salts!"

"Biddy, her smelling salts!"

"Where are they?"

"Up on her dressing table, probably!"

Biddy ran upstairs.

Mrs Erikson sat up and looked around her.

"Sally!" she said, as she gradually came to her senses. "Something terrible has happened. Look!"

She handed Sally the telegram.

> "Leaving school. On way to South Africa.
> Will write. Sam."

Sally read.

"What does it mean? How could he do this?"

"It means – it means he is going to join the army, to fight the Boers," said Sally. "Doesn't it?"

The situation in South Africa had been growing more dangerous all summer. By now huge English reinforcements had been assembled in the Transvaal, preparing for war.

"The stupid little fool!" Mrs Erikson's face regained some of its colour. "He is much too young to join the army. He will have to be stopped immediately."

Biddy came down with the smelling salts.

Mrs Erikson smelt them, and then said:

"Some tea. I need some tea. Where is Professor Erikson? He must go to England at once and stop Sam."

"Biddy, will you make some tea, with a lot of sugar?" asked Sally. "I think Professor Erikson is at work, isn't he?"

"Go and get him, go and get him immediately."

"He said he was going to the Library today." Biddy stopped at the top of the stairs. "He is down in the National Library."

"I'll fetch him," Sally said. "You go and lie down, Mrs Erikson. I'll fetch him."

Twenty-Two

Penny-farthing Sally

Sally got half a crown from Mrs Erikson and, throwing on her hat and jacket hurriedly, ran out onto the road. She planned to hail a hackney cab or a jaunting car but she stood for five minutes on the corner and didn't see a single one. She ran to the other end of the road, where the tram terminus was, but there was nobody at the tram stop and it looked as if she had just missed one. That meant another half an hour's wait.

She ran back to the house, and through the side door to the garden.

Five minutes later she was sailing down Palmerston Road on the penny-farthing bicycle.

Children stopped to stare as she passed. She sped along as fast as she could on the enormous, wobbling machine, but not so fast that she couldn't hear comments.

"Look! What is it?"

"Goodness me! I haven't seen the like of that since Noah built his ark!"

When she found herself on busier streets the comments became more numourous and more humorous.

"Windy up there Pet!"

"Can you give me a lift? I want to go to Mars."

"Where did that one drop outa? I thought them things was banned!"

Down Rathmines Road, over the canal bridge, down through Harcourt Street, Sally rode. The wind was with her and she sped along. Her hat blew off and her hair fell down from its pins, but she didn't stop. (She couldn't anyway, since the brakes on this bicycle did not work.)

Stephen's Green. The traffic was getting heavier all the time. She had to find her way around trams, jaunting cars, hackney cabs, private carriages. And other bicycles. There were lots of them but no bicycle that looked like hers.

Drivers called to her and cyclists rang their bells. Men whistled from the pavement. Her face was red from the effort of cycling, from the air on her face, and from embarrassment. But she felt more exhilarated than she had in a long time. So exhilarating was the journey that she almost forgot why she was making it, until at last she reached the little black gate in a wall in Kildare Street that said "LIBRARY". She cycled up to the railings, and by grabbing them managed to stop the bicycle. Then she flung herself off her high saddle, and was lucky enough to land on her feet. She left the bicycle lying against the railing outside the library, hoping that nobody would bother to steal it, and ran inside.

She found herself in a very big, empty, circular hall, with a marble floor and a high ornate ceiling. Several brown doors opened off the hall but all of them looked forbidding and she could see nobody at all. She walked across the marble to a wide staircase. When she was at the foot of the stairs a hand fell, gently, on her shoulder. She jumped.

"Can I be of any assistance?"

It was a little man in a black suit, very like the black suit the keeper in the park wore. But this man did not look like him. The park keeper had a big, pudgy, red face, with little hard eyes, whereas this man had a thin bony face, the colour of paper, and large, watery blue eyes, shining behind round black rimmed spectacles.

"Yes," said Sally, suddenly realising that she probably looked like a street arab or a tramp. Her hair was a complete mess, sweat was pouring down her face, and she hadn't paid much attention to what she was wearing. At least she had shoes on her feet. She caught him looking at them – the beggars on the street, who were very many indeed, usually did not have shoes.

"Yes," said Sally again. "I am looking for my employer, Professor Erikson. I have an urgent message for him."

"Very well," said the man. "He's in today all right. He's probably up in the manuscripts reading room. If you go up to the counter they'll fetch him for you."

"Thank you," said Sally. "Where is the counter?"

"Just go up those stairs. It's on your right as soon as you go in the first big door you come to."

Sally followed his instructions. She went up the wide, winding stairs, and into the big reading room of the libary. This was an enormous round room, with the highest ceiling she had ever seen. The room was full of long tables and at these tables men sat, reading books and newspapers. The thought flitted across Sally's mind that she would like to sit there too, and read all day in this quiet, solemn room. But there were no women at all to be seen.

"Can I help you?" A man spoke to her suspiciously from behind a high carved counter.

Sally explained once again.

"Oh yes," he said. "Professor Erikson. He's in today. Just a moment, young lady," he gave her a curious look and whispered something to a young boy sitting at a table behind him. The boy sprang up and walked quickly across the room to one of the tables where, Sally could now see, Professor Erikson was sitting, his head bent over a book. He glanced up when the boy spoke to him and nodded at Sally. Then he put on his hat and coat and came over to her.

They had to wait until they came out of the room to talk. Sally told him what had happened.

"I knew he would do something like this," said Professor Erikson. He did not seem at all as upset as his wife was.

"It is a great shock for Mrs Erikson," said Sally. "She was very anxious that you should know immediately."

"Yes, well, that is good. But I do not know what I can do about it. If he is gone he is gone."

They left the library and walked out onto Kildare Street. A hackney cab was waiting just outside the gate of the library.

"Ah," he said, "what good luck! We can take this, can we not?"

"I'm on a bike," said Sally. "Your wife's old one!"

It was still lying against the railings.

"Oh, you cannot ride that old thing," he said. "I will ask the driver to put it on the roof . . . "

"No no," said Sally. "It's all right. I like it. If you help me to get on, I'll cycle home on it."

"If you insist," he said, with a short bow.

He held the bicycle while Sally climbed onto the wall which supported the railings and mounted the saddle by that means.

"Goodbye!" she waved. The professor waved goodbye to her and got into the cab.

He was already home when she arrived, the horse being faster than the bicycle, at least a penny-farthing.

"Sush!" said Biddy. "She's at him to go after the young fella. And he doesn't want to go."

157

"That won't make any difference," said Sally cynically. "He'll go, all right, in the end. You wait and see."

"Oh sure, I suppose you're right," said Biddy. "The missus wears the trousers in this house and no mistake."

Sally went to her room to tidy her hair and wash her face. Then she decided to find out what was happening.

She knocked on the door of the drawing-room and went in.

"Is Snow here?" she asked. "We need to study a little."

"She is not here," said Mrs Erikson, explosively. "And how could she possibly study at a time like this? I need you to help Erik to pack. He is going to Southampton immediately, to try to put a stop to this nonsense."

"Can't you contact the police and ask them to help?" asked Sally.

"No. We don't want the police to get mixed up in our family affairs. Then it would get into the newspapers and I simply could not bear that!"

"Oh," said Sally. "I see."

"Could you go up to the attic and fetch a carpet bag down, please?" asked Mrs Erikson. "Biddy will show you where they are, if you don't know."

"Certainly," said Sally. "But where is Snow?"

"How would I know?" said Mrs Eirkson. "She has probably run off to Gretna Green, to get married, or somewhere else. She's probably gone to the north Pole to meet a polar bear. What children! What terrible children!"

Sally and Biddy found their way into the attic and got out a few big bags. Then they selected what they believed would be an appropriate wardrobe for Professor Erikson on a short trip to Southampton and packed all the clothes in one of the bags.

"Do you think we should bring it down to him?" asked Sally.

"Oh indeed and I do," said Biddy. "The sooner the poor man gets on his way the better it'll be for him and all of us. Bring it down straightaway and I'll get his coat and hat for him."

Sally went back to the drawing-room with the bags.

"We've packed," she said.

"How very kind of you," said Mrs Erikson. "Off you go, Erik, and don't come back without him!"

"Oh dear, dear, dear," said Professor Erikson. "Oh dear, dear, dear! I must get some books to read on the way. Where am I going?"

"You're going to Kingstown to catch the mailboat. Then you're going to Southampton."

"I am going to get some books as I said, Violet," said Professor Erikson firmly. "The mailboat will not leave until six o'clock. Please telephone for a hackney. I will not stand on the side of the street waiting for one."

"Very well," said Mrs Erikson. She went out to the hall and cranked up the telephone. Within half an hour, Professor Erikson had left. The house felt strangely empty, and there was nothing to do all of a sudden. Mrs Erikson did not want dinner. Snow came into the kitchen and had some bread and milk. Sally and Biddy were left alone, by the fire.

"Do you think he will find him?" Sally asked, idly. She knew Biddy did not know that answer any better than she did.

"No, devil a find," said Biddy. "Sure the young fella has to do what he wants to do anyway. Isn't he seventeen years of age or more?"

"Still, it is young to go to a war . . . "

"Indeed and it is not. And all them young fellas like to be warring and fighting. It's in their blood. I never knew a young fella didn't like fighting."

"Sam has such strong feelings about South Africa. In a way it doesn't surprise me that he is trying to go, now that war seems likely and English reinforcements are being sent out there."

"Well, at least there is no war yet. Maybe there will be none," Biddy sighed.

Twenty-Three

A Night on the Town

Professor Erikson sailed for England that night.

Mrs Erikson felt a little better when he had gone.

"At least I feel we are doing something!" she said. "Perhaps he will get to Southampton in time to stop Sam from sailing. What I can't understand is how any regiment would let him join up without getting his mother's permission!"

"Sam is seventeen," Snow said. "Maybe they don't think you need your mother's permission when you are seventeen. Do you think he will be shot?"

"Sh, Snow," said Sally. "We don't even know that he has left as yet. Of course he won't be shot. Anyway, the English side is much stronger than the Boer."

"The British have five hundred thousand troops, and the Boers fifty thousand," Thomas told her, the next evening. They were on the tram, going into town. "If he had gone to fight on the Boer side I could understand it."

"He feels very British," said Sally. "He thinks the English have been doing their best for the Africans."

"He is very naive if he thinks that," said Thomas. "They

are really interested in it because of the gold and diamonds."

"Well, he thinks there is more to it than that," Sally said. "Anyway I don't think it makes any difference to the Eriksons which side he wants to be on. They just want him to come home."

"No doubt that is how the families of all the soldiers feel," Thomas smiled. "But life must go on. War must go on."

"Must it?"

"I think so. It does, anyhow, doesn't it? One war followed by another. It seems to be an inevitable part of life."

"Mm," said Sally. They were sitting inside in the tram; it was cold and getting dark. Autumn was drawing in.

"Where are we going?"

"I thought the Royal," said Thomas. "There is a show on – *London Ways* – it is supposed to be very good. Have you been to the Royal before?"

"Never," said Sally. "That sounds very pleasant. I will be glad to see it."

So far, this engagement with Thomas was proving very easy.

That is how Sally had expected it to be. But Biddy had been alarmed.

"You're going out with a young gentleman?" Biddy was incredulous at first. She stood at the range, stirring a pot of chicken broth, which Mrs Erikson believed would help to soothe her nerves.

"Thomas. I've often gone out with him before," Sally said breezily.

"I never did see the like of you, Sally. I never saw a servant girl who consorted with the upper crust the way you do. No good will come of it," she nodded sagely, giving the soup a mighty stir. "When young men like that go out with young girls like you, there's only one thing they have in mind."

"I'm much too canny for anything like that, Biddy, and well you know it!" Sally laughed, biting into a raisin scone.

"I know it but does he? I don't know who's leading who up the garden path but I know this much: no good will come of it. You should stick with your own kind. Like with like, that's what I say."

"Well, maybe I just don't agree with you there, Biddy," Sally sucked in her cheeks.

"Maybe you don't, but you will. Mark my words. There's a natural order to these things. It was all planned by the good Lord above. Everyone has his or her place in the world and it's better that they stay there. How would it look if the good old queen came in here and started frying the rashers for us?"

"She looks as if she fried plenty of rashers in her time," said Sally. "She has that rashery look to her, I think, Queen Victoria."

"You are a great one for arguing," Biddy clapped the lid on the pot and sat at the table. "But no matter what you say, you'll find I'm right. Isn't there some lad up there in the back of beyonds where you come from that would be good enough for you?"

"No," said Sally. "Ne'er a one. Isn't it sad?"

"It is surely," said Biddy. "Sure look who's talking? An old maid and no mistake. When I was young I was too good for any that would have me and now who'd take me?"

"I'm sure there's plenty would be glad of you, Biddy," Sally protested.

"Indeed and if there is I don't ever meet them," said Biddy. "I'm on the shelf now and that's a fact. How will it be if I die an old maid in the garret? Sure I am in a garret and I am an old maid."

"Ah, don't be talking like that," said Sally.

The doorbell rang.

"That'll be him now!" she said. "I'm off!"

"What time will you be in at?" called Biddy after her, as she ran up the back stairs.

"Ten o'clock," shouted Sally.

She opened the door before anyone else could get to it.

"Sally! You look delightful," Thomas smiled with pleasure.

Sally had taken some care with her appearance. She was wearing her favourite dress, her lilac and white pinstriped lawn, with a lilac sash. She had a black jacket over it, and a jaunty black hat with feathers which Mrs Erikson had given her.

"Thank you," said Sally.

The show in the Royal was different from the plays Sally had seen before. It was a comedy, about the snares of life in the city for a young lady. It was full of jokes and songs, and during the intervals a troop of dancers wearing white bloomers and glittering tops laughed and kicked their legs high in the air.

Sally had never seen women displaying their legs in public before. She found it all embarrassing.

The audience, however, enjoyed the whole thing immensely and shouted and clapped loudly whenever an item they particularly appreciated was performed.

It was all very warm and lively.

"Is it always like that?" Sally asked Thomas, as they stepped out into the dark.

"Sometimes they throw rotten tomatoes," said Thomas. "It depends. Tonight's performer was very popular. They love him, in Dublin."

"I see," mused Sally. There were still so many aspects to life in Dublin that she knew nothing about. She glanced around her, at the street robed in the velvet soft night – she loved it like this, with the lamps glowing like candles, the shop windows gleaming gently in the dark like smooth lakes of glass. Even the people you saw in Dublin at this time were different from the daytime crowds – younger and more beautiful, well-dressed, happy.

"We never went to the Coombe, or to Cook Street," she followed this train of thought.

"Only because you ran off to Donegal without telling anyone about it," joked Thomas. "We can still go to those places whenever you have time, if you still want to."

"Oh, I do, I do," said Sally eagerly. And it was true. She wanted to see the places in Dublin which were probably very like the places Katie had lived in in Glasgow. Imagine being able to go and see them as a sort of tourist, though, while her own sister had lived in such misery! How odd life was!

"Would you like to go now?" he asked.

"Well, it is a bit late, isn't it?"

It was ten o'clock.

"We can walk along one or two of the streets in question," Thomas said. "It won't take more than five or ten minutes. Of course if you'd rather not . . . "

"No, no . . . I'd like to," Sally said a bit nervously, peering into the darkness.

Thomas led her along Dame Street as far as Christchurch Cathedral.

"We can go up this way," he said. "You'll see Patrick Street, and Cook Street, and then the Coombe."

The cathedral loomed, dark and sombre, like a great mountain, behind them, as they turned into a dark warren. High houses, all with steps up to the doors, lined narrow streets. There were bins on the footpath and the smell was appalling.

"It's not so different from other places," Sally said.

"It is different from Palmerston Park though, isn't it? No gardens, no trees, no space. Come here . . . "

He led her up a flight of steps to a black hall door. He pushed the door and it opened.

"Should we?"

"Nobody knows, or cares," said Thomas.

They found themselves in a big hallway, the same size and shape as the hall in the Eriksons' house. But there the resemblance ended. The hall was cluttered with old rusty perambulators, bicycle wheels, and broken teachests. There was no covering on the floor and the walls, which had once been painted, were dank and damp. The place smelled of rotten mushrooms.

"If you went into those rooms, you'd find ten or twelve people living in every one of them," said Thomas. "There is probably one tap in the backyard to provide all the people in this house – maybe more than a hundred – with water, and one toilet out there."

"The smell is appalling."

"You can guess why."

A man came into the hall. He was middle aged and shabbily dressed.

"What are yez doin' here?" he asked. A smell of drink was added to the other smells in the hall.

"Are yez lookin' for somebody?"

"No sir," said Thomas.

"Yez'd better be off so," said the man. "Yez are trespassin' on private property."

"We're just going," said Sally. She and Thomas got out of the house as quickly as they could, onto the dim, eerie street. They walked quickly back towards the cathedral. Sally heard footsteps behind them. The man had come out again and was watching them from the foot of the steps.

"Who are yez?" he called. "Would yez like a cup of tea?"

Sally shouted back

"We've got to catch a tram!"

The man waved to her and smiled.

"Maybe you would like a cup of tea," Thomas said, when they were back on the well-lit, fashionable streets. "Or a glass of wine? We have time. The last tram is at twenty past eleven. There is a nice place – the X and L café."

"I told Biddy I'd be home at ten."

"Does it matter that much? Have you a key yourself?"

"No," said Sally. "But I can get in."

There was a key left, all the time, under the bootscraper outside the hall door.

"In that case . . . ?"

Sally thought of Biddy's warnings. She looked at the café interior, visible through its curtained window. It looked warm and inviting. She looked at Thomas, in a soft black suit, snowy white collar and floppy black tie.

"All right," she said. "That would be lovely."

They sat in a little red velvet snug. Thomas had a glass of beer and Sally a cup of tea.

"It's not a public house, is it?"

She knew if she ever entered a public house her reputation would be lost forever. It would be almost as bad as having a baby.

"Oh no, I'd never bring a lady into a public house. Are you mad?"

"No. But perhaps you don't think I am a lady."

"I know you are a lady, Sally. All my female friends are. It is axiomatic."

"Aha. But you know nothing about me."

"You keep saying that. I think I know what I need to know. But tell me about yourself."

It is never possible to answer that question well, and Sally was no better than anyone else at it.

"Well, I suppose you know all the important things, as you say," she said. "I'm from a farm in Donegal. My father is

167

dead and my mother has married again. I've a sister called Janey and then Katie, who is sick."

"How bad is she?"

"She is not getting any worse. I think she may recover."

"If she has consumption it is not likely . . . "

"Oh," Sally was shocked at the bluntness of this. She felt as if someone had thumped her in the stomach. "I don't think she has consumption, really."

"I beg your pardon, I wasn't thinking," Thomas said. "I had got that impression, somehow. Well, I am glad to hear that she is better. It must be a relief to you."

"It is," said Sally. "But now we have this other trouble. Sam and the Boers."

"That is not your trouble, precisely," Thomas looked away.

"No. But I live with the Eriksons. I am involved with everything that happens there."

"It must be strange, living in a family which is not your own."

"I am used to that," said Sally. "The family feels like my own while I am with them."

"And then you leave?"

"And then I leave," agreed Sally. "But, of course, sometimes people like me do not leave. They spend their whole lives with one family."

"Yes. Would you like to do that?" Thomas looked at her curiously.

"No," said Sally, feeling confused. "No, of course not."

"So what do you think will happen to you, in the future?"

"I don't know," said Sally. "How could I know? I have to take each day as it comes."

"I'd find it very hard not to have some plan," Thomas said. "Would you like some more tea?"

"Thank you," Sally sat back in her plush seat, suddenly

feeling very tired. Thomas's words had opened up an unattractive vista for her – long years of living at second hand, in other people's homes. It would be like living on the edge of life all the time, instead of being in it.

"You look upset," said Thomas. "I haven't upset you, have I?"

"Oh no," Sally lied. His voice was so soft and full of concern. Sally looked at him. He had a pleasant face, and in many ways was a charming young man. But he had a disarming quality of tactlessness about him. He seemed to have a knack of finding people's weak spots and targeting them. She admired his directness and honesty but a certain abruptness, made him hard to be with.

"Perhaps you would like to have a family of your own, Sally?" He interrupted her reverie with this question, which took her by complete surprise.

"Well," she laughed. Shouldn't they be going home? "Yes, I suppose everyone would like that . . . "

"I would," said Thomas. His face flushed and his eyes glowed.

"Will you marry me, Sally?"

Twenty-Four

Ladysmith, Mafeking and Kimberley

Sally had had no real proposals for most of her nineteen years, and now she had had two within the space of a month.

It would have been easier, she felt, to deal with one at a time.

Sally did not give Thomas an immediate answer. She had not given Manus an immediate answer, either. He had written her a few letters since she had come back to Dublin, but in none of them had he repeated his proposal to her. Perhaps he was being true to character, not knowing whether he wanted her or not?

The atmosphere in the Eriksons' house was not conducive to decision making.

Mrs Erikson was constantly on edge with anxiety about Sam. Professor Erikson reported from Southampton, by letter or telegram. But the reports were far from satisfactory. He could not find Sam, or get any information about him. Although he had checked with army headquarters, they had no record of a Sam Erikson signing up with any regiment.

"Probably used a false name," said Snow cheerfully. "I think he will be eaten by a lion."

"Oh Snow, do not be so utterly heartless," Mrs Erikson was reclining on the sofa in the drawing-room, sipping weak tea. The doctor had been with her many times and had prescribed opium, so she was often in a dreamy and transcendent state. "Lions. Poor Sam, terrible to be fed to the lions. Are there lions down there?"

"I don't think so," said Sally. "I think they are further north, in Africa. South Africa is very far away. Sam won't have reached it yet even if he has got on a ship. It takes about eight weeks."

"That is a comfort. Maybe the whole skirmish will be over by the time he gets there."

War had broken out and was being waged fiercely. Even though the Boers were heavily outnumbered, their knowledge of the countryside and the terrain helped them in their fight against the British. During October and November they had the upper hand, and there were plenty of British casualties.

Each report of further battles in the newspapers upset Mrs Erikson.

At the end of November Professor Erikson came home, much to everyone's relief. Although he sometimes seemed scattered and vague, he was a rock of common sense by comparison with Mrs Erikson. As soon as he walked in the door the household felt more solid and content than it had in weeks.

"Sam has sailed," he said, as soon as he was in the drawing-room.

"I can't bear it!" cried Mrs Erikson. But she did not faint. She sat on her chair and waited for more information.

"He joined an Irish regiment, the Dublin Fusiliers."

"I'm surprised he demeaned himself!" said Snow.

"Yes. They did not have a record, at first, but that was an

oversight. He used his own name. He joined at the end of September, and sailed soon after that."

"Couldn't you get him back?"

"I can't stop a ship once it has started, dear," said Professor Erikson. "I am as sad as you are, but there is nothing we can do now but hope and pray for the best."

"When will he arrive – is he there already?"

"The voyage lasts about eight weeks. So he will arrive soon, if he has not already done so. I have sent letters to the regimental headquarters in Cape Town, asking him to contact us immediately."

"A letter must take eight weeks, too," said Mrs Erikson.

"Yes, but he can telegram information. He may do that," said Professor Erikson. "We can but hope."

Two weeks later the Boers had great victories, and besieged the towns of Ladysmith, Mafeking and Kimberley. There were many more British casualties. The Eriksons became more anxious than ever, as there had been no word at all from Sam.

Twenty-Five

Season's Greetings

It was a few days before Christmas.

Dublin was gaily decorated for the season.

The war in South Africa affected some families, since there were Irishmen fighting on both sides. The city was colorful with recruitment posters and lively with anti-recruitment marches. Many Irish people, like many people all over the world, were sympathetic to the Boers, who were proving themselves to be brave and heroic in the face of huge forces from the greatest empire in the world.

But most Irish families were unaffected. For them, the Boer War was a distant trouble. It was the stuff of newspaper headlines, but not anything that struck at the heart of their own lives. The citizens of Dublin prepared enthusiastically for Christmas. It would be an exceptional Christmas, since it was the very last one of the eighteen hundreds. The New Year would literally usher in a new age – the twentieth century. It was impossible not to feel a certain excitement at the thought. The nineteenth century had brought great changes to the world – steamboats, trains, bicycles, the telephone. The very latest invention, the motor car, was so new and amazing that people could not yet believe that it would ever catch on. Still, it was there. A few Daimlers and Mercedes could be seen already on the streets of Dublin, chugging bravely along among the horses and trams. What unimaginable wonders of technology would the twentieth century bring? What advances in civilisation?

The Eriksons made some attempt to prepare for Christmas. They had not heard from Sam, but nevertheless had gradually become accustomed to the idea that he was gone, and that he was taking part in the war. Knowing which Regiment he belonged to was a blessing. At least it was better than knowing nothing at all about him.

Sally helped with the preparations, decorating the house with holly and ivy, buying presents with Mrs Erikson and Snow. Shopping still cheered Mrs Erikson up, even though she was, in general, miserable.

Sally continued to see Thomas. She had told him she needed time to consider his proposal, that the upheaval at the Eriksons made it difficult for her to know what to do.

He was not very happy with that. Naturally, he wished she would know immediately that he was the only man for her. Sally wished she could have known that too.

The truth was, she liked Thomas, and had been mildly attracted to him for a few months. But as soon as she had met Manus again her old feelings had reasserted themselves. And it had seemed that Manus had been determined, at last, to follow the arrow of his own feelings for her. But so far nothing had actually happened.

Manus had a bad record: he had demonstrated, in the worst possible way, that he was weak and easily influenced by other people's opinions. He had preferred to hurt another – to hurt Sally – rather than face discomfort himself.

But that had all been a long time ago. When she had last seen him he had seemed contrite and even desperate.

Maybe he had changed completely over the last few years? Maybe he had grown up?

How could she know this? She couldn't, not yet anyway, until he had time to prove himself. Would she be a fool if she gave him the benefit of the doubt before that time? Or would she be a fool if she did not do so?

The only thing she was certain of was that she was attracted to him as, she believed, she could never be attracted to anyone else. She still liked the way he looked, the way he talked, the way he moved, more than she liked any other human being. She liked the way he smelled – of fresh air and flour and soap – and the way he screwed up his nose when something puzzled him.

When she thought about it, at four o'clock in the morning, in the dark depths of December, it seemed to her that what she felt for Manus was what all the stories and romantic novels recognised as true love. Every part of Manus gave her pleasure, just to think of or remember. When she was with him she felt more complete than at any other time. She was happy. It was enough, it was all she wanted, it was, she knew, a foretaste of heaven.

But the fly in the ointment was that she did not trust him, and with good reason. Would she be a fool to forgive and forget, to give him the benefit of the doubt? Or would she be a fool not to?

Thomas had not blotted his copy book in any way. The perfect gentleman, he had always struck her as being naturally kind and unselfish, a young man who was totally reliable and would be supportive and considerate always. She enjoyed his company. He was sophisticated and knowledgable, and would teach her many new and exciting things. He had done this already, in the short time she had known him. He would bring her to new, wonderful places. With him she would inhabit a brave new multi-coloured

175

world: Dublin with its theatres and bookshops, its poets and revolutionaries, its talk and music, would be the stuff of her everyday life. She would travel, perhaps, to places which she had only known from the pages of novels, to London, to France and Italy, to the great places of the world.

She did not feel about Thomas as she felt about Manus. With Manus, she felt as relaxed and easy as a baby in its mother's arms, whereas with Thomas she was watchful, a little bit edgy. But that was perhaps because she did not know him very well as yet?

She lay on her flat white pillow, and the pale grey morning light slowly leaked into her room. Sally racked her brains, trying to find the right answer, the best and perfect answer – an answer which she feared did not, alas, exist.

It was a relief to get up and pull on her clothes, even though she felt worn out after the night's tossing and turning. Sitting at the big kitchen table, eating one of Biddy's warm new-baked breakfast rolls and sipping a cup of hot sweet tea, was delightful. A sense of repose overcame her. The copper pans hanging on the wall, the row of blue and white plates, the china mugs, on the dresser, the black range with its glowing saffron fire and its array of cauldrons and kettles, were a joy in themselves. Ordinary things, the ordinary routines of the day, were comforting, after the great romantic drama which was playing at top speed in her head.

"Did you ever fall in love, Biddy?" she asked. Biddy was sitting opposite her, digging into a big plate of rashers, eggs, sausages and tomatoes.

"What sort of a question is that to be asking at this hour of the day?" Biddy speared a sausage with her fork and began to carve it up into bitesize pieces.

"But did you?"

"Indeed and I did. Everyone does that sometimes."

"So, what happened?"

"Nothing, nothing at all. Otherwise I wouldn't be sitting here, would I? I'd be sitting in some other kitchen. Probably not a very good one."

"Did he not know?"

"He knew. But nothing came of it – it couldn't have."

"That's sad, isn't it?"

"It is not. It was all for the best."

Biddy buttered her roll with satisfaction.

"Sometimes young girls think it's the end of the world when these things don't happen. But it's not. Life goes on all the same, and in the end the only thing that matters is if you have a clean bed to lie in, and enough food to fill your belly."

"I suppose so," said Sally, turning to her own food. She couldn't agree with Biddy, and not only because she was younger than her. Ordinary things, material things, like food and beds and heat, were important, but surely they could not be the only thing that mattered in somebody's life?

"My religion is a great consolation to me," said Biddy, reading her thoughts. "I have a great devotion to the Sacred Heart. When I feel worried or anxious about anything I go down to the chapel and say a little prayer and light a candle at the shrine of the Sacred Heart, and then I feel better."

"Ah yes," said Sally. "I know what you mean."

In the middle of the afternoon, while Sally was in the nursery with Snow, reading, the doorbell rang. A few minutes later, Biddy called to Sally from the bottom of the stairs.

It was Manus.

He stood in the hallway, twisting his hands.

"Manus, what are you doing here? Is something wrong?"

"Nothing is wrong," he said. "I had to see you."

Biddy was standing under the stairs, observing and listening, but she couldn't understand a word of what they were saying.

"Oh, well, how did you get here?"

Sally stalled, not knowing what to say to him. He was wearing a thick tweed jacket, in a nubbly mixture of white and brown, and black frieze trousers. He had a white shirt which didn't fit very well and a bow-tie that had been bought in a shop sometime, but maybe twenty or thirty years ago. The cap he held in his hand was a funny shape. His socks were white báinín and he wore big boots. In this hallway he looked like a freak.

He looked like a country bumpkin, in town for the day.

He looked like what he was.

"Manus!" Sally felt a surge of sympathy for him. Poor Manus! he had never been to Dublin before, he didn't know a thing about it. She gave him a quick hug, aware that Biddy was not far away.

"Manus!" she said again. "It is great to see you. Come with me and we can go somewhere and talk in a few minutes."

She brought Manus down to the kitchen – Biddy had reached it just seconds ahead of them, and stood by the range, trying to look as if she had been there for ages.

"This is Manus, Biddy. Manus, Biddy," Sally introduced them

"Oh yes, Sally's young man from the country," said Biddy, with a smirk.

Sally sat him down and gave him a cup of tea. Then she ran back upstairs to Snow.

"Snow," she said. "Manus is here."

"That funny man from Donegal?"

"Yes. He has come down to see me about something important. What's funny about him?"

"He has sticking out ears," said Snow, patting her own, which were small and neat as shells.

"Oh? I'd never noticed," Sally dismissed this thought. "I'm

going out with him for a little while now anyhow. Biddy will be here with you. Is that all right?"

"Of course," said Snow. "Can I see him?"

"Yes, yes," said Sally impatiently. "Go down to him while I tidy myself up a bit."

Sally and Manus went for a walk in the park.

The black-clad keeper was there, walking around telling boys to stop kicking balls and girls to be careful on their tricycles. He stared at Manus when he saw him, and gave Sally an inquisitive look. It was not often that tweedy Donegal farmers went for a stroll in his prim and proper park.

Manus told Sally all the news about her family. He had called in to see them just before he left, and had a letter from her mother. Sally read it quickly – Katie was still well, she read, and hopeful about the future. The doctor had called again and had given her some medicine, and he too continued to be hopeful. She did not ask if she would come again, but Sally could read between the lines.

Sally pointed out features of the park, and asked Manus if he would stay for long.

"Until the New Year," he said.

"You'll spend Christmas in a guest house? And the New Year?"

"The new century. I'll see the twentieth century in in a guest house in Dublin, if necessary. I'll stay as long as necessary," he said.

"Necessary for what?"

"For you to make up your mind," he stared at the ground.

"Oh, that!" said Sally.

"Will you?"

"Manus, you know I love you more than anyone else, don't you?"

"No. But good, if so."

"But . . . I'm still not sure."

"When can you tell me? Just tell me, one way or the other. If you don't want me, I'll go away and never bother you again. I promise."

"I'll tell you tomorrow, Manus. I promise you that much."

They walked silently along the raked path. Sally brought him to the rose arbour and the garden of statues.

"Look!" she pointed at the statue of the centaur. "Do you see that, half man and half horse? Once I was lost in here at night, and I thought it moved and smiled at me."

She went up to the centaur and stroked its curly hair.

"It looks a bit like you," she said. "Although when I first saw it I was so frightened that I thought it was a woman."

"Thanks very much," said Manus, glancing down at his hobnail boots. "Nobody has ever mistaken me for a woman before."

"It's worse to be a horse, I'd say," said Sally.

Twenty-Six

Black Horse, White Horse

It was the twenty third of December, two days to Christmas. That was the day when Mrs Erikson received her first communication from Sam.

A letter, which he had written as soon as he had arrived in Cape Town, came in the afternoon post.

Dear Mother, Father and Snow,

You have probably wondered what has become of me over the past months? Or perhaps you have found out. I am in Cape Town, a junior officer with the Dublin Fusiliers, and looking forward to defeating the enemy with all due speed.

I know you will have been very anxious and I apologize from the bottom of my heart for what I have done. But I hope you can understand why it seemed necessary. I realised if I asked for your blessing I would not get that. And I also realised that the most important thing in the world for me was to offer my services to my queen and country.

I have had a comfortable voyage from Southampton

to the Cape. Tomorrow my battalion travels from here
to Spion Kop, in the Northern Cape.

I have never been happier or healthier in my life.

I send you all my fondest affection, and look
forward to the time when we will all be together
again."

In great haste,

Your affectionate son,

Sam.

"When we will all be together again . . . ? It is so
touching – " Mrs Erikson was crying. "But we could all be
together now!"

"You still have me," said Snow, putting her arm around
her mother.

"And me!" said Professor Erikson. "And it is clear that
Sam has done what he wants to do. We must grant him the
freedom to be his own man."

"It is so hard to be without him!" said Mrs Erikson sadly.
"I love him so dearly. I hate to think of him out there in that
hot, terrible place."

"Let us make the best of it," said Professor Erikson. "Let
us have a happy Christmas, for Sam's sake!"

Thomas called to see Sally later that afternoon.

"Sally!" he smiled his gentle smile when he saw her. "You
look tired . . . "

"I am," she said, wanly. "I didn't sleep last night, and it
has been a long day."

"Do you feel like going out?"

"No, and I don't think I can anyway. I am supposed to
be looking after Snow. Biddy has gone shopping."

"Can I stay here for a bit?"

"Of course."

They sat in the kitchen, the only room in the house which Sally felt entitled to use for her own visitors. Even when the whole house was empty, as it was tonight, she could not sit in one of the main rooms. What a restricted life it would be, to be a servant forever, like poor Biddy! Even if you had a two roomed cottage it would be better than this, if it was your own.

Thomas sat and chatted about this and that for half an hour. He told Sally he would go out to Bray the following day to spend Christmas with his parents, and asked her if she would like to visit them too?

"It is time I introduced you to them," he said. "They should have that privilege, if we are going to be married."

Sally started back from him.

"But we haven't made any definite plans," she said.

"I thought we had," said Thomas, still smiling.

"But I never said . . . anything."

"No, I know, my dear. But of course since we have been together so much, I have presumed to take that as an affirmative reply."

Sally put her hand on his wrist. Her expression told him what he needed to know.

"Thomas. You have misunderstood. I am sorry. But I had not made up my mind."

Thomas's face grew white.

"And," Sally continued, "Someone has come to see me – from home."

"Some man?" Thomas stared grimly at her. His face looked bleak and accusing.

"Yes."

"For God's sake, Sally, what are you playing at? You told me there was nobody else."

"There wasn't. Not really," Sally raised her eyebrows.

"Not really? What the devil does that mean? There either is or there isn't."

"I wish it were as simple as that!"

Thomas banged his cup down on the table and stood up.

"I've offered you everything, Sally. I've offered you myself. Do you think it's easy for someone in my position to marry a hired girl?"

"No," said Sally, quietly.

"You're damned right it isn't. My parents may be poor but they're not illiterate peasants. What do you think they will say when I tell them about you?"

"You said that it would be fine."

"Of course I can do it, I can persuade them that it is all right, and it doesn't matter anyway what anyone thinks. But my friends. Imagine introducing you to my colleagues in the department. One of them is marrying the boss's daughter. Another is married to the daughter of a judge."

"How extraordinarily clever of him!" said Sally coldly.

Thomas knelt at her feet.

"Sally! None of that matters to me. I'm just saying, I was prepared, I am prepared, to sacrifice all kinds of things if you will have me. And what do you do? You play around with my feelings as if I were a messenger boy or a farm labourer."

"I'm sorry, Thomas. I just need time to make up my mind. I need to do that, as much as anyone, as much as a queen or a princess or a judge's daughter would, even if I am only a hired girl."

"Oh Sally, Sally! I'm sorry." Thomas was in tears. "I didn't mean all that. I'm just so angry. Who is this fellow anyway? Where is he?"

Thomas looked as if he would murder him if he could set eyes on him.

"His name is Manus. He's just an old friend from home. He'll go back in a day or two."

"Alone?" Thomas snarled cynically.

"I don't know. I'm being honest with you. Now if you'd be good enough to leave me for a while . . . I'll see you tomorrow."

"Goodnight, Sally. Don't test me too far!"

Thomas went out and slammed the door.

Sally heard the white horse whinneying. Over the sounds of the city and over the sounds of the country, its cry called. She saw the black foal straining at the traces, breaking free. She saw it dashing over the purple mountain, its hooves pounding, pounding against the turf as it raced. It galloped to the ridge of the hill. The whinnying was louder. The black horse stood on the rock and saw the white mare reaching out for it from the deep, black lake.

The black horse gave a mighty leap, into the middle of the dark lake.

The whinneying stopped.

A calm settled over the water. It rippled gently, softly, it plashed against the reeds. The sky was cloudless, silver blue, quiet as the depths of the ocean. The wind caressed the lake like a touch of a gossamer web.

Sally felt a great peace descend on her.

She knew what she would do.

She put on her coat and hat and set out for Manus's hotel.